one plus
two

Edited by: Three Owls Editing

Cover by: Jess Mastorakos

Formatted by: Christina Butrum

To my readers who fell in love with Maple Glen...
Welcome back

Chapter One

THE LAST THING HANNAH EXPECTED WAS TO be stranded on the side of the road, in the middle of nowhere, with a baby in the backseat.

Had she known the car wouldn't be able to handle the five-hour drive, she would have figured out another way.

Holding back tears of frustration, Hannah turned the key in the ignition, willing the car to give it one more go and get them safely to point B. She silently prayed to a higher power to help her out of this mangled mess of a situation she'd been thrown into involuntarily.

When the car refused to turn over, she slapped a hand against the wheel and bit back a sharp cry as she leaned her head against the steering wheel. She didn't know a thing about cars, except how to check the oil, which she had done before leaving her apartment in Chicago.

She glanced over her shoulder and checked the backseat. Thankfully, the baby was sound asleep and Hannah's frustrations and whispered prayers hadn't woken her.

The sun was setting off in the distance, and the snowflakes appeared to have doubled in size. Heavier flakes landed against the windshield and melted instantaneously. It wouldn't be long before the heat in the car vanished and the chill of the evening air crept in.

She needed to do something, but she wasn't quite sure what she could do other than call for help. But who could she call? Her best friend was still more than three hours away and would be expecting Hannah and the baby.

Reaching into her purse, Hannah retrieved her phone and sent a message to let Tara know that she and the baby wouldn't be arriving anytime soon. She quickly added that she was on the side of the road in a town called Maple Glen—according to her phone's location.

She set the phone down next to her and turned the key in the ignition. The whir of the motor thrummed to life, but the car refused to stay running. She thought about popping the hood and taking a look, but with her niece in the backseat, she didn't feel comfortable leaving her alone in the car—it didn't matter if she would be right outside or not.

But then again, Hannah was at a loss for options.

As though her prayers were answered, headlights shined brightly through the back window of her car. She squinted against the brightness reflecting off the mirrors and silently hoped that it wasn't a serial killer.

Within seconds, her mind raced through several scenarios, and in response she pressed a button to lock the doors. She watched in silence as a man climbed out of the truck behind her and made his way up to the driver's side door of her car.

He shined a flashlight into the car and offered a friendly smile as he peered inside. She hesitated a minute before taking a chance. She grabbed the handle for the window and cranked it down a crack.

"Hi there," the man said, offering another friendly smile and a kind wave of his hand, "are you having some car trouble?"

She glanced in the rearview mirror and noticed two other occupants in his truck. One of which appeared to be a woman, though the other was hard for Hannah to make out.

"Unfortunately, yes," Hannah replied, breaking her eyes away from the rearview mirror and turning her attention back to the friendly man.

"Do you have anyone on their way to help you out?" he asked, glancing back to his truck, which made Hannah look in the rearview mirror once more. When she shook her head in response to his question, he said, "Give me one second."

Before Hannah could say a word, the man walked back to his truck and said something to the passengers. Her phone chimed beside her, alerting her to an incoming text message. More than likely it was from Tara, who without a doubt was worried about them.

She kept her eyes on the man as she reached for her phone. Sure enough, Tara was asking what had happened, if they were okay, and if she needed to come to the rescue.

Hannah smiled at the thoughtfulness of her best friend but quickly replied to the message with an update. *I'm not sure what happened, but the check engine light—*

A soft knock on the window pulled her attention away from her phone. She glanced up and the man motioned for her to step out of the car. "Cassie's calling her brother to come out and help," the man explained, taking a step to the side while making sure she had plenty of room to get out of her car. "You're more than welcome to come and sit in the truck while we wait for Carter to get here with the tow truck."

His offer was sincere, but she couldn't afford a tow truck. She had just enough money to cover the expenses of the last-minute trip to Tara's.

The man stopped and turned back toward her, realizing that she wasn't following him. She looked in the backseat through the window and couldn't believe the unraveling of events. Everything had seemed to be going well with her sister and her new bundle of joy. Little did Hannah know that her sister had struggled to accept motherhood and would end up leaving the baby in her care without a single word as to where she was going or what was going through her mind.

Tears of frustration and sadness stung Hannah's eyes as she opened the back door and reached in for the most precious gift God could ever offer. She unlatched the buckle and lifted her niece out of the seat, pulling her close and wrapping the blanket around her small body to shield her from the chill of winter.

Hannah took a step away from the car and shut the door. She had no choice but to take the man up on his offer and sit in the warm truck. She was more than thankful for the assistance as the wind nipped against her nose. It would have been only a matter of time until the heat dissipated in the car.

"Thank you," Hannah said, stepping to the side as the man opened the back door for her and Grace. She climbed into the backseat and was pleasantly surprised to find a bright, blue-eyed girl no more than seven or eight staring back at her with a smile on her face. "Hi," Hannah said with a smile, thankful to learn the chance that these people were serial killers was slim to none. "Thank you so much for stopping."

"No problem," the little girl said, taking it upon herself to peek under the blanket at Grace. "We love to help everyone. That's what makes us good people," the little girl said proudly with an even wider smile on her face. "I'm Alexandria, but everyone calls me Alex. So you can, too."

"Sounds good. My name's Hannah," Hannah said, relieved by the little girl's kindness. Out of all of the scenarios that had played through her mind, not one of them involved a friendly family of three coming to her rescue. She smiled, knowing God was listening to and answering her prayers. Even if they hadn't been answered instantaneously, Hannah was trying her best to be patient.

"What's the baby's name?" Alex asked, peering over the blanket and stealing another glance at baby Grace who was now wide-eyed and content with the little girl's attention. Hannah didn't know a thing about taking care of babies, but so far, Grace wasn't much fuss. She was a quiet and calm baby—only crying when she needed her diaper changed or wanted a bottle.

"Her name's Grace," Hannah answered, dismissing the realization that she left the diaper bag in the backseat of her car. She made a mental note to grab it before her car was towed away. The thought of getting lucky and the car starting once the mechanic showed up crossed her mind, but she knew it was wishful thinking.

"Well, I'm Cassie," the woman in the front seat said, offering a kind smile and tucking a loose strand of hair behind her ear. "I'm not sure if Grant told you, but my brother, Carter, is a mechanic and will be here any minute with the tow truck."

Hannah nodded as she swallowed past the lump in her throat. In Chicago, the cost of a tow truck ranged from a hundred dollars to an arm and a leg. It all depended on mileage and the time of day.

The silence was interrupted when Grant opened the driver's door and climbed inside. "I popped the hood, and aside from the cloud of smoke, I couldn't see anything wrong," he said, glancing over his shoulder with a subtle shrug.

"My brother's good at what he does," Cassie assured Hannah. Hannah nodded, taking her word for it. She didn't know the town she was in, let alone the people who lived there. She only hoped that it wouldn't cost her too much to get her car running again and back on the road. "Speaking of which... there he is now."

Hannah twisted in her seat when headlights lit up the cab of the truck and saw the tow truck pull in behind them.

"Alex, you stay put, okay?" Grant said before climbing out of the driver's seat.

"Okay, Dad," Alex answered, smiling at Hannah while giving her father a friendly salute.

Hannah smiled and grabbed the handle with her free hand. She gave the door a gentle push and snuggled Grace against her chest before climbing out of the backseat.

She could only hope that Carter was as good as these friendly strangers proclaimed him to be and she would be back on the road in no time.

Chapter Two

CARTER GRUMBLED AND MUMBLED AS HE shifted the tow truck into park behind Grant's truck. He had just gotten off work an hour before and had tossed a frozen pizza into the oven when his phone rang.

But, he wouldn't turn down an opportunity to make a quick buck or two, and once he hauled the vehicle back to the shop, he would be on his way home to eat. His stomach growled as though it could understand his thoughts, causing him to let out a subtle grunt before climbing out of Ol' Toad and making his way over to the stranded car and motorist.

"What have we got?" he asked no one in particular as he approached the tail end of Grant's truck.

A woman with a bundle of blankets in her arms stood off to the side and offered him a shy 'hello' as he came to a stop next to her.

"That's your car, I take it," Carter asked, pointing a finger in the car's direction.

"Yes, it is," the woman said, releasing a sigh as she switched the bundle around in her arms. Only when she switched from one side to the other, he saw the baby. He hadn't ever seen the woman or child before, which made him wonder what brought them through Maple Glen. He shook his head, clearing the questioning thoughts running through his mind. It wasn't any of his business. "I was driving along the road here and the check engine light came on, so I pulled off to the side and that's when it just died."

He nodded once before taking a step toward the car. "Mind if I take a look? It might just be somethin' simple. You can go ahead and hop in where it's warm. There's no sense in standing out in the cold with a baby," he said over his shoulder as he made his way to her car. Grant met him at the front of the car. "You sure it isn't out of gas?"

Carter's question was supposed to be funny, but no sooner had the words left his mouth, than he heard a throat clear behind him. His eyes widened at the realization that the owner of the car had followed him. He shot a look at Grant, but he was on his own as Grant offered nothing short of a slight chuckle.

Carter turned around and was met by a mad glare. He had a feeling that she didn't find his question too funny. He tried to offer a quick apology, trying to right the choice of words he had used, but she wasn't having it.

"I'll have you know that I can read a gas gauge," she said. "I'll also have you know that it has just under a full tank."

Carter gripped the back of his neck and adjusted his stocking cap, pulling it down over his ears. There was no doubt that he had offended her—and rightfully so. The last thing he needed was an upset customer. He had spent time earning his keep in Maple Glen as a mechanic. He couldn't allow one disgruntled customer to make his reputation flounder. No matter if he deserved it or not, he needed to apologize and make it right.

"I'm sorry," he said sincerely, and whether or not she accepted, he meant it. "I didn't mean for it to come out the way it did. It was supposed to be a joke."

The woman stared at him, keeping up with the glare and refusing to cut him some slack. "I checked the oil before I left Chicago..."

Her words trailed off and he could almost sense the regret she felt for possibly saying something that she didn't want him to know. "Chicago, huh? What brings you all the way over here?"

He should have let it go. He had no right to ask questions like that, but honestly, he had grown up in Maple Glen, and it had the small-town way of living. People knew everything about everyone—whether they liked it or not. He was more of a stay-to-himself kind of guy, but it didn't hurt to ask a few questions every now and then.

"Oh... just... we... "

He didn't have to look at her to know that she was nervous. He heard it in her voice before she cleared her throat for the second time that night. He held up his hands, offering to let it go. "It's not my business... I'm sorry," he said, quickly turning his attention back to the stranded car on the side of the road and away from the woman with a baby in her arms. He took a look under the hood, shining his flashlight around the engine and looking for anything unusual.

He couldn't see anything that would explain the sudden stall, but then again, it was getting darker by the minute and he didn't have all the tools he needed to take a better look. Without saying a word, he opened the driver's door and slid into the front seat. He turned the key in the ignition and, sure enough, the car had plenty of gas but refused to turn over.

"Well?"

The woman hovered over the door and peered in at him. The baby was asleep in her arms as she studied him, waiting for him to tell her what? Good news? He wouldn't be able to give her that. Not tonight at least.

"Well," he said, climbing out of the car and taking a step backward. He would have to pull his truck around and line it up evenly with her car in order to hook it up. "It's got a full tank of gas."

He offered one of his well-known grins and was

relieved when she let out a slight chuckle. "I'll have to take it to my shop across town and have a look," he explained, hooking a thumb over his shoulder. When she didn't say anything, he said, "I won't be able to do anything with it tonight, but I can start on it first thing in the morning."

A look of defeat crossed the woman's face as she pulled the sleeping baby closer to her chest. He didn't know what the woman's situation was, or where she was even headed, but it didn't take a genius to figure out that she was stressed.

"If you need a place to stay—"

"I don't think staying with you is a good idea," she said, quickly cutting him off. He should have been taken aback that she thought he was implying that she stay with him, but instead, he found it amusing.

"My sister, Catie, owns a bed and breakfast just down the road a ways," he said, finishing the sentence with a smirk. It might have been well after dark, but he could see the redness in her cheeks as she turned away.

"Sorry," she murmured, obviously embarrassed by her assumption.

"Apology accepted," he said. "I'd say we're fairly even now?"

She smiled with a nod, and he took the minute he had to introduce himself before he got busy with hauling her car to his shop. "I'm Carter Mitchell, by the way," he said, extending his hand and feeling awkward for wanting to shake hands with her. But she accepted and said, "Hannah Michaelson."

"Alrighty then," he said, releasing her hand and immediately feeling the loss of warmth her hand had provided his. "Do you have a phone number I can get?"

"Strictly business," he quickly added, holding his hands up in surrender to ward off any negative assumptions the woman might have made when requesting her number. He could only laugh it off when she nodded and asked, "Do you have a pen and a piece of paper?"

He patted his pockets and realized he had emptied them when he arrived home for the night. His usual routine once he arrived home at night included discarding anything unworthy of impor-tance out of his pockets and kicking off his steel toed boots before grabbing a cold one out of the fridge and showering.

"Not on me," Carter said, glancing back at the tow truck, "but I think I've got one in the cab of my truck. One sec."

He jogged to the tow truck and debated on whether to drive it and park it where he needed it, or hurry back with just a pen and paper in hand. Deciding it was better not to waste any more time, he climbed into the truck and shifted into drive. He kept the truck idling as he crept along the road, making sure not to hit anything or anyone as he pulled up in front of the broken down car and shifted into park once again.

Carter climbed out of the cab and almost forgot to grab a pen and paper before hopping to the ground. "Here you go," he said, offering them to her. She took a hold of the paper and fumbled with the baby in her arms. He watched her furrowed brow as she tried her best to write her number on the piece of paper. "Want me to hold him so you can write?"

He wasn't quite sure where the question came from, but he couldn't just stand there and watch her struggle. It had been a while since he'd held a baby, but he was confident that he could manage a quick minute or two.

She let out a nervous laugh and carefully handed the baby to him. "*She*'s quite the handful," she said with another subtle laugh before clicking the pen and scribbling on the paper. He didn't mind holding the baby. Actually, the warmth from the blanket alone warmed his hands, and when he looked down, wide eyes were staring at him. He chuckled when the baby's face scrunched in confusion. "I think she's wonderin' who the heck I am," he said with a chuckle. "She's not so sure about this, Mama."

Hannah turned without acknowledging what he'd said and handed him the paper. "Thank you" was all she said before taking the baby from his arms and heading toward Grant's truck.

Carter wasn't sure what that was all about. He

hadn't said anything wrong. He was just making conversation and light of the situation.

He watched as she cradled the baby close to her and climbed into the backseat of Grant's truck. Carter hadn't thought to talk with Cassie about checking with Catie, but if he knew Catie, she would have room for two at the bed and breakfast.

And even if she didn't, there was no doubt in his mind that his sister would make room for them. With the comfort of that thought, he folded the piece of paper she'd given him and tucked it into the pocket of his flannel jacket.

Carter took a minute and made sure the car was ready for him to tow it. When everything was lined up and ready to go, he hooked onto the metal frame and secured the broken down car to his tow truck before hauling it to his shop and calling it a night.

Chapter Three

HANNAH LOOKED OUT THE BACK WINDOW AS Grant pulled away from the side of the road and headed in the direction of the supposed bed and breakfast owned by Carter and Cassie's sister. Hannah had almost forgotten the car seat in the car, and if it hadn't been for Grant, she would still be holding tightly to the infant. Thankfully, he thought to grab the suitcases and diaper bag as well. She really needed to get used to having a plus-one.

Instead, her niece was buckled in safe and sound while being entertained by a cheerful little girl sitting beside them in her booster seat. Hannah smiled when Alex glanced over at her. Her heart melted at the interaction between the two girls, which allowed the overwhelming thoughts she'd had earlier to dissipate.

Hannah wasn't sure what to expect next. Other than needing to focus on getting her car fixed and back on the road, she couldn't do much at the moment, anyway. She would take it one day at a time while praying that everything would work out in the end.

The silence in the cab of the truck was interrupted intermittently with Alex's giggles as she played peek-aboo with the baby. Hannah's thoughts ranged from getting to the bed and breakfast to how she would pay to get her car fixed.

"So, you're from Chicago, huh?" Grant asked, looking at her in the rearview mirror and interrupting her thoughts.

"Yeah," she replied, thinking first before saying too much. "Born and raised."

Grant nodded, and Cassie took over the conversation. "What brought you this way? Do you have family here?"

Cassie's question was nothing short of polite, but Hannah wasn't sure what she could say that wouldn't give her away. Not that she was ashamed of what happened back home, but she didn't know these people from Adam. She would keep her answers relatively simple and her personal life guarded for the time being.

"Well, we were actually on our way to my friend's house," Hannah replied, motioning toward Grace. "Tara—my friend, that is—just had a baby herself, and she thought it would be great to get the two together while catching up over coffee."

It wasn't a complete lie, but they didn't need to

know that. Once Grant and Cassie had come to her rescue, Hannah had made it her mission to pull off the whole "new mother" act. Whether or not it was believable would be determined soon enough.

"You like coffee?" Cassie asked, a smile spreading across her face as she turned sideways in the front seat to face Hannah. Hannah didn't just like coffee, she loved it. She lived on coffee. It was a staple in her house, and it fueled her twenty-four seven.

"My Aunt Fran owns a coffee shop here in town," Cassie said without waiting for a response from Hannah. "I can take you there tomorrow if you'd like."

Before Hannah had a chance to say anything, Grant intervened. "I don't know if that's a good idea."

Hannah caught sight of his smirk in the rearview mirror and looked to Cassie for an explanation. Cassie rolled her eyes and shook her head, waving it off like it was no big deal. Hannah wondered who Fran was and why it wasn't a good idea that she meet her.

"Don't listen to him," Cassie said, "Fran's a wonderful woman, and I'm sure the two of you will get along just fine. There are no strangers in Maple Glen as far as Fran's concerned."

The explanation was reassuring, but Hannah still felt a bit uncertain about meeting the woman, or any of the people in Maple Glen. She just wanted her car fixed and to be back on the road before anything else happened.

"I'm just saying," Grant said, trying to turn the

conversation back to the point he originally tried to make. Hannah wasn't sure she wanted to hear what he was saying.

Thankfully, Cassie cut him off yet again with a stern look. "She isn't *that* bad. You're going to scare our guest away before she even gets settled, Grant."

Hannah shook her head and offered a friendly wave of her hand. "Oh, no, that's okay," she said, "I think I'll just stick around the bed and breakfast until my car is fixed and ready to go. I don't want to intrude on your time by having you—"

"Nonsense," Cassie said with a slight chuckle. "I have all the time in the world."

Hannah couldn't imagine the kind of life that could possibly exist where people had enough time. She couldn't ever find the time she needed to take care of the things she had to get done. She glanced down at Grace and realized she barely had time for the baby, let alone anything else.

"Well, at least until dance class, anyway," she quickly added with a wide smile on her face. She turned back toward Hannah and said, "That's where we were tonight. I own the barn out by where your car broke down."

Hannah nodded. She hadn't seen a barn, but then again, she hadn't been paying attention to much else other than the check engine light and being in the middle of nowhere.

"I remodeled it and turned it into a dance studio

for my ballet classes," Cassie explained, glancing back at Alex— who sat up at the mention and nodded her head enthusiastically. "I'm going to be a ballerina when I grow up," she said with wide, hopeful eyes.

Hannah didn't doubt her statement for one minute. She had only just met the girl, and she could tell she had a knack for something special.

"Well, here we are," Grant said, guiding the truck into the driveway belonging to the bed and breakfast. Hannah let out a relieved sigh. "Cathryn's Bed and Breakfast."

The house sat back from the road a ways, and if its looks were anything to go by, it was going to be a decent place to stay for the night.

Hannah grabbed the car seat and struggled to unhook the base from the seatbelt. Grant stepped in and lent a hand, telling her to go on ahead and he'd help carry in her belongings. She couldn't thank him enough for being so helpful. That went for Cassie as well.

A dog barked as a sensor light flipped on. Hannah froze at the sight of the large black lab barreling toward them. She wasn't afraid of dogs, but then again, she never had one running straight toward her either.

"Duke!" a man shouted from somewhere on the porch by the front door. "Come, boy!"

For a split second, Hannah thought the dog would listen, but he proved her wrong as he continued on his mission toward her. She kept her feet planted and protected Grace the best she could with the majority of her body.

"He won't hurt ya," the man said, walking down the steps and heading out to the driveway. "He just gets excited when we get company, is all."

"Yeah, that's the truth," Cassie said, walking up and standing next to Hannah. "Ask Catie about Duke's first few week's here."

Hannah gripped the car seat tighter as Cassie guided them toward the house. The lab was now being controlled by the man he'd refused to listen to as they walked past them. The man introduced himself as Ethan.

Hannah smiled politely and offered a friendly 'hello' as she followed Cassie and Grant onto the front porch.

The screen door flung open, and a woman mirroring Cassie's resemblance stepped outside to greet them. "You must be Hannah?" she asked, offering a smile as she looked down at the car seat. "And Grace, right?"

"Yep, that's us," Hannah said with a smile. "I hope that we're not imposing on anything tonight."

The woman waved it off and said, "I'm Catie, and I assume you've already met Ethan and Duke?"

Hannah glanced over her shoulder and said, "I sure have. That dog is huge."

Catie laughed and reached for the screen door before

holding it open for everyone as they entered the house. "Tell me about it," she said, walking in behind them. "I keep telling Ethan that we need to stop feeding him bacon, but the darn dog loves it too much, and I wouldn't put it past him to get depressed if we take it away."

Hannah raised a brow, wanting to know more, but Catie waved it off and said, "Long story. We'll save that for tomorrow."

Grant walked in with his hands full and set everything down at the foot of the stairs. "I've prepared a room for the two of you," Catie said, taking hold of Hannah's things and motioning for Hannah to follow her upstairs. "I hope you don't mind décor from the early twenties, but the room is ideal for a mother and child."

Hannah followed her upstairs, biting her lip as she carried Grace. She wouldn't correct anyone who assumed Hannah was Grace's mother. That was best for now. They wouldn't be staying in town long enough for them to care, anyway. Soon enough, Hannah and Grace would be on their way to Tara's, and she wouldn't have to worry about keeping things to herself.

"I'm sure it'll be just fine, thank you," Hannah said, trailing right behind Catie to a bedroom door off to the right of the staircase. Catie opened the wooden door, and Hannah was more than impressed with the room. "Wow, this is beautiful."

"Thank you," Catie said, placing Hannah's stuff on the end of the bed.

"Our grandmother owned this house while we were growing up," Cassie said as she walked into the room. "Catie had her heart set on owning it one day and dreamed every night about turning it into a bed and breakfast."

Hannah set the car seat down and unbuckled Grace. Lifting her out, Hannah said, "To be honest, I would have loved to have my grandmother's house after she passed away."

"I couldn't let a house full of so many childhood memories go to waste," Catie admitted, glancing at Cassie with a smile. Hannah knew all too well what that felt like, but she wouldn't chime in about it. Her childhood had been full of fun and precious memories... until it wasn't.

She shook her head and cleared the thoughts from her mind. She held Grace close to her chest and inhaled the sweet baby smell, which led to an uninvited yawn.

Hannah quickly snapped her mouth shut and apologized. Cassie and Catie waved off her apology. "Don't be silly," Cassie said. "You've had a long day. I'm sure you're ready for bed."

She looked at Catie then back to Hannah. "I know I would be."

They nodded in agreement before Catie said, "Is

there anything I can get you before we head downstairs?"

The thought of something to eat crossed Hannah's mind, but it was too late and she didn't want to impose.

"Have you had anything to eat? I can make you something quick," Catie offered. "Or how about some hot tea or whatever you'd like to drink?"

Hannah smiled at Catie's hospitality. There was no doubt that Catie had chosen the right dream to chase when it came to running a bed and breakfast. She was on top of making her guests feel welcome, and Hannah was thankful for that.

"Tea and a quick bite to eat sounds wonderful. Thank you," Hannah said, laying Grace down on the bed for just a minute as she unzipped her bag and pulled out pajamas for both of them.

Catie and Cassie turned to leave the room, but Hannah wouldn't let them leave without one more thanks. They both paused by the doorway and smiled back at Hannah. "It's our pleasure," Cassie said. "See you downstairs?"

Hannah nodded. "I'll be down as soon as I get the two of us changed into something comfy for the night."

Turning her attention back to the pajamas she had placed on the edge of the bed, Hannah smiled down at Grace. Her niece cooed and squealed as Hannah tickled her sides. She didn't know a thing about raising a child, but she would try her best to make it work. Hannah refused to let her niece end up in the foster care system just because the child's mother decided to walk away.

It pained Hannah to think about her sister abandoning Grace, but the alternative would have been a lot worse. At least now, Grace was in Hannah's care and she wouldn't have to worry about her being left hungry or all alone in an empty apartment building.

Shaking the thoughts from her mind, Hannah grabbed the outfit she'd picked out for Grace to wear to bed and placed it beside her.

"What do you say we get changed and head downstairs?"

Hannah picked Grace up and carefully changed her into cute, footed pajamas with baby elephants. Grace was content with her aunt's choice as she plucked at the tiny elephants and hearts lining her pajamas, cooing and babbling on like the six-month-old baby she was.

"My turn," she said to the baby who was now lying on her back and watching Hannah struggle into her own pajamas. She had opted to bring her own footed pajamas along, knowing Tara would get a kick out of the matching duo. But Hannah hadn't thought about the impending complications of trying to get her feet into the stockings.

Stumbling across the wood floor, Hannah reached out for the side of the bed and missed it completely—

falling and causing a commotion loud enough for everyone downstairs to hear.

Grace must have thought Hannah was playing around, because no sooner had she tripped and fell over her own two feet, than Grace let out a shriek of joy and her eyes lit up. Hannah shook her head and pushed herself off of the floor.

Plopping down on the edge of the bed, she focused on getting her other foot in and adjusting the pajamas before zipping them up. She chuckled at the thought of how hideous she must look and considered changing into something else.

But, then again, the people downstairs might get a kick out of the matching pajamas and find them absolutely adorable, too.

"Are you ready to go downstairs, Grace Lynn?" she asked, lifting the baby off the bed and carrying her to the other side of the room. "Here goes nothing."

She took a deep breath and opened the door leading to the hallway. For all they knew, she was the mother and she didn't have a crazy life waiting for her back home. *Home.* She honestly didn't feel like that was the right word to use to describe the two-bedroom apartment she and her sister had been living in.

It was far from the kind of home that Hannah had imagined. Especially at the age of twenty-three. One would think that she would have a good paying job and, not to mention, be engaged or something.

Isn't that what twenty-three-year-olds were

expected to have nowadays? A good-paying job and a committed relationship?

She laughed at the thought and stepped into the hallway. Living in a city had its pros and cons, but Hannah didn't have time to list them. She just knew that she needed to get out of there and find something better for her and Grace.

She had been well on her way until her car decided otherwise.

Chapter Four

CARTER HAD SLEPT WELL FOR A CHANGE, AND he was more than ready to put in the work that awaited him at the shop. But, first things first, he needed to stop into Fran's Coffee and grab himself a cup to go.

Much like his brothers, he didn't take time to visit his aunt. He knew that Fran hated when they didn't stick around and chat, so he would apologize like all the other times he'd done it and be on his way.

He hated to think about what Fran would say when she found out about the woman and baby being stranded in Maple Glen. His aunt was known for a lot of things in Maple Glen, but nothing topped her reputation as being the queen matchmaker.

He chuckled at the thought as he climbed into the cab of his truck and turned the key. The truck rumbled to life with a slight hesitation. Carter kicked the defrost on and waited a few minutes before backing out of the driveway.

He hated winters as much as the next person, but he had to admit he enjoyed riding his snowmobile on the trails by the river. Not to mention taking an afternoon off from the garage and going ice fishing.

Carter thought about taking a few days this coming week to head out on the lake but quickly remembered he had Deputy Bradley waiting on him to finish up on his SUV. He couldn't leave the Sheriff's Deputy without a vehicle for too long— no matter if he had a back up or not.

The thought of Hannah's car crossed his mind. He had to fix her car, too. But that would take a lot longer than Vince's SUV considering he needed to figure out what was wrong with it before he got too carried away with making promises of when he'd have it fixed and ready to go.

He pulled into an empty spot out front of his aunt's coffee shop and shifted into park. He thought about taking a few extra minutes with his aunt just to make her happy as he hopped out of his truck.

It had been a while since he'd had a decent conversation with Fran. Usually, he was working on cars from sunup to sundown. He could never find the time to break away unless he had his part-timer step in and cover for him.

Speaking of which, he needed to give the kid a call and ask him to fill in mid-week so Carter could head to the lake. He would have Vince's SUV done by then, and there was no doubt that the kid could fix Hannah's car.

He smirked at the idea. That would get him out of seeing her again. Not that he disliked her. It was the complete opposite. The way she'd stepped right up and put him in his place when he'd offended her... and the way she protected that baby of hers...

He spit the chewing tobacco out of his mouth and entered the small-town coffee shop. The sleigh bells above the door announced his arrival as he stepped inside. It didn't take Fran long to lock eyes on him and hurry over to him.

"Where have you been?" Fran asked, patting him on the back as she wrapped her arms around him. She gave him an old-fashioned bear hug, squeezing him like she hadn't seen him in years.

"I've been at the shop," he said. "It's been busy there."

"So I've heard," she said, letting go and taking a step back. "What's this about a woman and a child being stranded on the outskirts of town?"

Carter figured his aunt would have heard all about it. It didn't take long for word to travel in a small town like Maple Glen. Especially around the coffee shop. "Less than twenty-four hours ago and you know all about it, huh?"

Fran offered a subtle shrug and scurried off behind the counter. "I don't know *all* about it, but I've heard a few things here and there," she said, giving him one of those looks that told him he was pressing his luck. "What can I get ya to drink?"

"I need a—"

"Let me guess," she huffed, "you want your usual to go, am I right?"

Carter took a step back and raised his hands in defense. "Easy, killer," he teased, but that didn't help matters. She furrowed a brow and pointed a finger at him. He surrendered with a light chuckle and said, "Okay, I'll stay, but only for a minute or two."

"That's my boy," she said, pulling a cup from the stack and heading for the coffee pot. "Go ahead and have a seat. I'll bring it out to ya."

Carter didn't have to be told twice. Fran was his mother's sister, and he knew when to listen. If his aunt wanted company, it was in a person's best interest to stick around.

He took a spot by the window only to realize that his sisters, Cara and Cassie, were chatting over coffee with Autumn and Emmalee. He caught their attention with a quick wave and politely refused their offer to sit with them. He didn't get into that whole "coffee shop talk with the girls" thing.

He'd thought Cassie would have brought Hannah since she loved being the one to introduce newcomers to the town's offerings. But then again, he was thankful that she hadn't because there was no doubt in his mind that Hannah would ask about her car.

Even though, to be fair, he had been the one who told her that he would work on it first thing in the morning. Well, it was morning, but he wasn't going to be working on it.

"Here ya go," Fran said, placing his cup in front of him and sliding into the chair across from him. "So..."

He took a drink and quirked a brow. "So..."

Fran placed her elbows on the table and leaned forward. "What's this Hannah girl like?"

Carter should have known that his aunt would ask twenty questions about Hannah, but he also knew nothing about her so his aunt was out of luck.

"I don't know," he said, and took another drink from the steaming cup. "It was dark."

Fran scoffed and rolled her eyes. She leaned back while shaking her head. "Dark schmark," she mumbled, crossing her arms in front of her. "Did she say where she was headed or how long she'll be in Maple Glen?"

"Aunt Fran," he said with a stern look on his face. He didn't know anything about the new woman, and he wasn't sticking around just to talk about her. "I'm not working for the Sheriff. I don't ask twenty questions while helping a stranded motorist."

Fran furrowed a brow and leaned in close once again. "Well maybe you should. We'd know a lot more about her."

Carter shook his head and leaned back. He scratched a hand over his stocking cap and thought about taking it off, but decided against it because that would give Fran the impression he was enjoying the interrogation... or that he was sticking around for it.

"Why do you need to know about a woman who's just passing through?" he asked, pulling at the sides of his cap. He would be heading back out in the cold soon enough and didn't want the cold wind nipping at his ears.

"What if she's running from a dark past? Or an abusive boyfriend?" Fran asked with wide eyes. "Or what if she secretly needs help and has no one to turn to?"

Carter couldn't help but let out a loud laugh. "Oh, come on, Aunt Fran. Cut it out. This isn't one of those murder mystery shows you always watch."

Fran scoffed again, crossing her arms in front of her as she rested them on the table. "What if it is, and I'm right?"

Carter shook his head and glanced at the clock on the wall. "I don't know, but I really need to get going."

"Well, I guess I'll just have to see for myself then, won't I?" Fran asked him as he slid out of his chair and stood up.

He knew no matter what he said, the woman would figure things out on her own anyway. That's just who Fran was. There would never be a time when Fran didn't know the happenings of the small town or who was coming and going.

Carter glanced over toward Cassie who was giving

him a funny look. He debated turning the spotlight on her for once, making it known that Cassie actually spent more time with this Hannah woman than him. He smirked at the thought and said, "Actually, you were supposed to meet her this morning, Aunt Fran."

Fran looked from him to Cassie and gave him a puzzled look. He pointed at Cassie and said, "If I'm not mistaken, Cass was supposed to bring her in this mornin' to meet you and have a cup of coffee."

His aunt registered what he was saying and no sooner had it clicked, than she was making her way over to the booth housing the women and starting in on her inquisition. "Someone's got some explainin' to do," she said just as Carter waved and headed out the door.

He would leave the women to bicker over who should have brought Hannah in for coffee and a meet and greet. He knew it wouldn't take long before Fran knew who Hannah was, but he didn't want any part of it.

Fran was full of it if she thought she would play matchmaker on his time. He didn't have any interest in all that love stuff, anyway. And besides, he had been there. Done that.

Carter stepped outside and pulled his stocking cap down further over his ears. The snowflakes were heavier than they had been the night before, making him wonder if there wasn't a blizzard on its way from the mountains.

Chapter Five

THE NIGHT HAD BEEN FILLED WITH PLENTY OF tea and laughter. Hannah and Catie were the last to call it a night, and even then, it had been well past midnight.

Hannah had tucked Grace into the crib upstairs in their room. She was beyond thankful that Catie and Ethan had a crib available for her to use. When she mentioned how grateful she was for the small things at the bed and breakfast, Catie told her the story of how the bed and breakfast came about.

She had listened with complete interest, finding it whimsical and a bit like a Hallmark movie—to which Catie had replied, "*That's what Ethan said!*"

The story about Duke had been the greatest—how the dog had chased the geese around the yard and Catie had burned the bacon.

Hannah hadn't laughed so hard in a long time.

Back home, nothing ever went the way Catie had described her life. Catie's life was full of love and hopeful dreams, whereas Hannah's was filled with the complete opposite.

She hadn't made the mistake of opening that can of worms while talking to Catie. Instead, she listened and pretended she could relate. Pretending was the best Hannah could do for now. For the time being, she would pretend to be Grace's mother—no matter how young she truly was or the label the people in town might give her for having Grace on her hip.

She couldn't tell anyone, including Catie, about her life back home in Chicago. She couldn't tell her that she didn't know what a home full of love felt like because her parents hadn't cared enough about anything other than their next bottles of booze and pills.

Hannah shook the thoughts from her head as she rolled over in the oversized bed. She glanced at her phone, checking the time, but also making sure Ashley hadn't tried calling her. A bright screen stared back at her. It was just after five a.m. and there wasn't one single missed call or text message.

It made Hannah wonder what Ashley was up to and why she hadn't cared enough to check on Grace. She had left the baby alone in the apartment, leaving Hannah in shock when she got home from working a ten-hour shift. No heads up. No note. Nothing but a cooing baby lying in a Pack 'n Play with a dirty diaper.

Hannah had called around, checking with friends the two of them had in common, but came up with nothing. She didn't give anyone too many details—especially none that would put a bad light on her sister.

She loved Ashley. Ashley was her older sister—her *only* sister—and she would never stop loving her or worrying about her, regardless of her recent decisions.

Hannah could only hope that when her sister realized they were gone, she would understand that Hannah was only doing what she thought was best for Grace.

Raising a child in the environment Hannah and Ashley had grown up in was cringeworthy. Hannah had mentioned it to Ashley several times, only to be told it wasn't her business. Many other times, Ashley confided in Hannah some of her deepest feelings and what all she was going through.

She recalled several times when she asked Ashley if she was truly ready to be a mother while her sister was pregnant. The pride and joy that had been written all over Ashley's face had fooled Hannah.

The thoughts made her upset... heartbroken. She had been tossing and turning all night in a bed so unlike her own, in a place that felt warm and welcoming, but still wasn't her own home. Which only allowed the thoughts and memories to taunt her even more throughout the early morning hours.

Hannah debated on trying to get more sleep or

head downstairs. But she didn't have the slightest idea what she would do once she was downstairs.

Usually when she couldn't sleep in, she would go out for an early morning jog, take in the sights and sounds, along with the fresh morning air that embraced her as she ran.

Jogging was out of the equation for today. She didn't know her way around Maple Glen well enough as it was, let alone to go jogging. Hannah was more than certain she wouldn't get lost, but then again, one never truly knew what kind of situation they could find themselves in.

Besides, she thought as she glanced over at a sleeping Grace, leaving the baby for any reason right now didn't seem like a good idea. Thankfully, the baby had passed the up-all-night stage and had settled in and adjusted well to the accommodations.

Hannah sat up in bed, scooted toward the headboard, and leaned back against the over-fluffed pillows. She would sit in bed for a while and figure out which step she would take next while waiting for the rest of the house to wake up.

Scrolling through her phone, she eyed her sister's phone number and hesitated for a minute before exiting out of her contacts.

She wanted to send a message to Ashley. She wanted to let her know that Grace was okay and with her for the time being. Hannah knew that it wouldn't sit well with Ashley, even though she was the one to abandon them—not the other way around.

A loud bark in the hallway, followed by a scratch at her door, pulled her attention away from the phone. She set it down on the nightstand and walked toward the door.

Another scratch followed closely with a low whine sounded on the other side as she reached for the door handle. "Just a minute," she whispered, cracking the door open just enough to see the black lab sitting right outside the bedroom. He whined once again, but this time he was pressing his nose against the wooden door and trying his hardest to barge into the room.

"What are you doing?" Hannah asked in a soft whisper. She held in her laughter as she opened the door the rest of the way. She allowed Duke to waltz into the bedroom like he owned the place—which he technically did, she supposed. "You're something else, you know that?" she asked the dog, but he ignored her as he made his way over to Grace. Her heart melted when he stopped next to the crib and laid down on the floor next to it.

"I'm sorry. He shouldn't have come in here like that," Catie whispered from the doorway in her flannel robe with a pair of bunny slippers on her feet. Hannah smiled and waved it off. "He's fine. He just wanted to check on Grace," she said, pointing to the dog who had found his spot and was now content.

"Are you awake for the day?" Hannah asked Catie,

hoping she would say that she was. She didn't want to sit in a quiet room any longer than she had to. She needed something to do in order to get her thoughts to settle.

"Yeah," Catie said with a smile. "Would you like to come down for coffee?"

Hannah nodded with a smile, feeling relieved that Catie not only offered coffee, but company as well. "Thanks, I'll be down in a minute or two," Hannah whispered, grabbing her phone once again. This time, she didn't hover over her sister's phone number too long before selecting it and sending her a message to let her know that everything would be okay and she would take care of Grace. She knew Ashley was going through a hard time with alcohol, and possibly drugs as well, but she could only hope for the best from here on out—for both Ashley and Grace.

She tucked her phone into the pocket of her pajamas and told Duke to keep watch over Grace. "Let me know when she wakes up, will you?" she asked with a smile as she patted the black lab on the top of his head before walking out the door and making her way to the kitchen.

Catie handed Hannah a cup of coffee and motioned for her to have a seat at the counter. Hannah gladly accepted the chestnut-colored drink with a smile. If she made it through the day without a nap, it would be a miracle. She only had herself to blame for the restless night of sleep as she allowed the thoughts to keep her awake. And it didn't help that she checked her phone several times throughout the night. Just in case.

She was more than positive that Ashley wouldn't respond to the message she had sent this morning. As far as Hannah knew, Ashley had bunked up with someone and couldn't care less about Grace and Hannah.

She certainly didn't care enough to keep the rent payments current. The eviction notice had been proof of that.

Hannah shook her head. She had been foolish to let her older sister take care of the bills. She should have known better than to give Ashley her hard earned money to pay half the bills without double checking that things were being taken care of.

"Is everything okay?" Catie's voice cut into the silence surrounding the two of them in the kitchen. Hannah looked up and feigned a smile. She hated when people asked that. It was the kind of question that made her want to break open and let go of everything she was bottling up inside of her.

"Oh... yeah... just tired and thinking about what could be wrong with my car, is all," she replied, not thinking twice about her response. "I still can't believe that it decided to quit on me."

Catie nodded, but remained quiet as she took another drink of her coffee. "Cars can be a pain sometimes," she finally said, "but I'm sure Carter will have it fixed and runnin' in no time."

Hannah smiled and appreciated Catie's assurance. She could only hope that Carter was as good as his sisters claimed him to be, and hopefully he would have Hannah's car back to her before waiting too much longer.

"I'm sure you've been asked this a dozen times already," Catie said, setting her cup down on the counter and glancing over at Hannah. Her eyes were soft and understanding, but also filled with curiosity. Hannah knew what she was going to say before she asked, "Where are you headed from here?"

"My friend, Tara, has invited Grace and me to her place for a week or two," Hannah replied confidently. She didn't have to lie to answer that question—no matter how many times she would be asked, it would be the same answer every time. "She's been wanting me to come for a visit for a while now."

Catie nodded with understanding. "Sometimes taking trips is hard to do. Especially with a little one."

Hannah brought her cup to her lips and took a slow drink. It was a sure way to take a minute to regroup and figure out how she could continue her charade of being Grace's mother. She set her cup down in front of her and said, "That it is. And then to think, I could finally take the trip and my car breaks down."

Catie's expression softened, and she reached out

patted Hannah's hand. "Everything will be just fine. You wait and see."

Hannah thanked her just as Grace let out a cry from upstairs. She glanced at the clock on the wall and was more than surprised the time had slipped by so quickly. "I'll be right back," she said, fumbling off of her stool and trying to make it out of the kitchen as Grace's crying grew louder. "I'm coming, honey. Just a minute," she called out, huffing it up the stairs and realizing it was going to take her some time to get used to taking care of Grace.

Chapter Six

CARTER FELT BAD FOR LEAVING THE COFFEE shop when he did, but he hadn't planned on sticking around for as long as he had in the first place. With a fresh cup of hot coffee in the console of his truck, he pulled into the parking lot at his shop.

He had thought of stopping by the bed and breakfast on his way by, but decided that it would make things awkward. They would want to know why he was stopping in, and he wouldn't have had an answer for them.

Besides the fact that he wanted to make sure Hannah would be able to pay him for fixing her car, he couldn't think of anything else he could talk about. But that didn't stop him from thinking about her and what had brought her to Maple Glen.

He shoved the key into the lock and unlocked the door. Stepping in, he did a quick scan to check for signs of life, but the place was empty and his part-timer was nowhere to be found.

He wondered if it was time to hire some new help. Maybe call on Ethan and see if he had some spare time on his hands. Carter knew that Ethan was busy learning the ropes of his grandfather's business, but there was no doubt in Carter's mind that Harold Davis wasn't planning to retire anytime soon—no matter what the old man said.

Harold Davis was a long-time business owner in Maple Glen. His business dated as far back as Carter's parents' meat locker and deli. Unlike Harold, Carter's parents had decided to retire and leave the business in the hands of his older brother, Clayton.

There was something about Maple Glen and owning a business in the small town. Being a business owner brought a sense of pride that a person couldn't find anywhere else. Sure, Carter could move his shop into a nearby city and make a lot more money than he was making now, but it wasn't all about the money.

At least, not until push came to shove and business was hard to come by. But so far, so good.

Carter glanced at the broken-down car that belonged to Hannah. He wouldn't have thought someone would be daring enough to take a long trip in an unreliable car, but he quickly recalled the time his sister, Cara, had driven into town with an old, rusted-out car, too.

He wouldn't curse that car of hers too much,

though. It got his sister back into Maple Glen, and it was a much needed family reunion. And, he was more than certain that Cara didn't mind being in Maple Glen once again. Not since she found the love of her life after receiving a parking ticket from him.

Carter cringed at the thought of finding love. He didn't care if love smacked him upside the face, he wouldn't fall for it. Not the way his brothers and sisters had fallen—thanks to their aunt Fran.

He made a mental note to steer clear of the coffee shop from now on. He could always make coffee at his place and carry it along with him to work in a Thermos.

His thoughts went back to his family and why he loved Maple Glen as much as he did. The Mitchell family was a close-knit bunch. There wasn't a lot that slipped through the cracks when it came to their family. It was one more thing Carter was proud of.

He glanced at the Coca-Cola clock on the wall and realized that the time wasn't slowing down or waiting for him to catch up. If he was going to talk to Ethan about coming and working with him at the shop, he needed to drive on over to the bed and breakfast now before Ethan headed out of there for the day.

Locking the shop back up, Carter shook his head at the thought of seeing Hannah. She would more than likely want to know why he wasn't working on her car, and he would have to tell her that he was working on it—just not at the moment.

He smirked at the scene playing out in his head. She wouldn't be happy with knowing that he was putting it off. He would just have to tell her that the world didn't revolve around her and that there were other vehicles in line ahead of hers. First come, first served.

Another smirk crossed his face as he climbed into the driver's seat of his truck and turned the key. The truck grumbled to life and sputtered against the cold. Carter gave it a quick pep talk, making sure his truck knew that he wasn't too fond of the winter months either as he shifted into drive and gave it some gas.

PULLING OFF THE ROAD AND INTO THE driveway leading up to his sister's bed and breakfast, Carter took in the sight before him. Ethan and Duke were out in the yard busying themselves with stringing Christmas lights around the evergreen tree centered proportionately in the middle of the property.

Carter shifted into park and killed the engine before hopping out of his truck. "Don't ya think it's a little too early for all that jazz?" he called out, shaking his head as he walked toward Ethan and Duke.

At the sound of his voice, Duke turned his attention from Ethan and barreled toward Carter. Carter braced for impact, knowing full well what the hundred-and-some-odd-pound dog was capable of. It wouldn't have been the first time Duke knocked Carter off of his feet, and he knew that it wouldn't be the last time either.

But Duke surprised him when he came to a complete stop at his feet and sat down. Carter looked up from the dog and asked, "What'd you do with Duke? This can't be the same dog."

Ethan shrugged as he hung the last of the lights on the north side of the tree. "Maybe he got bored with you," Ethan teased, walking up to Carter and offering him a pat on the back. Carter was impressed with how well Duke behaved sitting at his feet. It was only a few weeks ago that they'd had problems with him and the guests. Word had it that Duke had knocked a poor old lady off her feet who couldn't have weighed more than a hundred pounds soaking wet.

"Christmas lights already?" Carter asked once again, pointing at the display wrapped around the ever-green tree. He wasn't against decorating for the holidays, but he couldn't understand the rush... even if it was almost December.

Ethan shook his head and let out a low grunt. "You know your sister, bud. The moment Thanksgiving is over, it's the perfect time to start decorating for the season. And with it being so late this year, she wanted me to get started as soon as possible."

Carter laughed along with Ethan. He glanced up at the large Victorian home and was surprised to find it had yet to be struck with holiday cheer.

"You want to head inside?" Ethan asked, pulling his attention away from the lack of decorations on the house. "I've been out here a while piddling around with these lights. I could use a hot cup of coffee. What do you say?"

Carter went along with it. He figured it wouldn't hurt to have a conversation about the shop inside where it was warm. There was no sense in freezing. "Sure," he said, motioning for Ethan to go ahead and trailing right behind him toward the front porch. "I've got somethin' I wanna run past ya, anyway."

Ethan held the door for Carter, allowing him to enter the house first. Carter stepped into the front entryway and glanced around. There was no sign of Catie—or Hannah.

"I'm sure Catie has a fresh pot of coffee going," Ethan assured him, leading him down the hall from the living room and into the kitchen.

Carter heard her before he laid eyes on her. The smell of honeysuckle perfume lingered in the air surrounding her as he stepped into the kitchen and maneuvered his way around Hannah. He chose a spot to sit across from her.

"Hey, CarCar," Catie greeted with a welcoming tease. She had called him that since he had first learned how to walk. The nickname hadn't gone away over the last twenty years. "What's new at the shop?"

Carter swiped the plateful of leftover pancakes from the middle of the counter and gracefully coated them with maple syrup. He hadn't had anything to eat since the night before, and since then, he'd worked up quite the appetite.

He felt Catie's glare from across the counter. She stood with her back against the wall and her arms crossed in front of her. "What?" he asked, shoving a forkful of syrup-covered fluff into his mouth.

"You're such a pig," she chided, scrunching her nose at him and turning her attention to Hannah. "Please excuse my brother. Sometimes I wonder how it's possible we were raised by the same parents."

Carter set his fork down and dabbed a napkin against his mouth. Maybe he shouldn't have attacked the plate full of pancakes the way he had. Maybe he should have asked to make sure no one else wanted some.

"That's fine," Hannah said. Her voice barely above a whisper as she sat across from him without judgement. Carter grinned and turned his attention back to Catie. "See... not everyone thinks I'm a pig."

Hannah's laugh caught him by surprise. "I wouldn't go that far."

Carter's eyes fell on hers, and at that moment he noticed there was something about her that he hadn't from the night before—a hint of attraction. He shook the thought away as he debated on a good comeback, but he had nothing.

"Did the cat get your tongue, CarCar?" Catie teased, jabbing him in the side with an elbow as she made her way around the kitchen. She took his plate and scraped the remaining food into the garbage disposal.

"Not at all," Carter said, righting himself on the barstool and preparing to defend himself against the two women in the kitchen. "So... Ethan... as I mentioned outside," he said, changing direction in conversation and hoping it would take Hannah's eyes off of him. There was a magnetic pull—a tension he could feel and was trying hard to avoid it. "I've got a long line of cars needing repaired at the shop, and I could really use another set of hands."

Ethan glanced over at Catie before looking back at Carter. He hitched a thumb in her direction and said, "I'm all for it as long as the woman is okay with it."

Carter watched his sister as she made her way over to Ethan and wrapped her arms around him before sitting on his knee. If Carter wasn't interested in whether she would give Ethan the okay or not, he wouldn't have stuck around for the mushy stuff. His siblings made him sick with all of that.

As far as he was concerned, love was overrated. There was no sense in it. Trouble. That's all it was.

"He acts like I crack a whip around here," Catie joked, causing Hannah to laugh once again. Carter couldn't deny the fact that he enjoyed hearing Hannah laugh. There was something about the ease of tension as she relaxed against the counter. She had been so uptight when he'd met her...

"It's okay to crack a whip every now and then," Hannah said, clanking her coffee cup into Catie's.

"That's right," Catie said with a smirk as she took a drink of her coffee. "Us girls have got to stick together."

If Carter hadn't been paying attention, he would have missed the look that crossed Hannah's face at the mention of sticking together. The look of defeat, mixed with a bit of worry or disappointment, made him wonder what thoughts were going through her mind.

He quickly changed the subject and tried to get Ethan on board with working at the shop as a part-time fill in. "I know that you know your stuff about vehicles," Carter said, continuing on without giving the guy a chance to say no. "Honestly, I think I'd only need your help from now until the holidays are over."

Ethan studied Catie's reaction, and Carter could only hope she wouldn't be upset if he pulled Ethan away for a few hours a day. Catie smiled and said, "I'm okay with that. I think I can manage hanging a few decorations up around here by myself."

"Do you know what's wrong with my car yet?" Hannah asked, eyeing Carter from across the kitchen as she poured herself another cup of coffee.

He had known she would ask about her car. He had figured out the perfect response, but of course, being put on the spot with her eyes staring into his, he lost all train of thought and everything he'd planned to say went right out the window.

"I... uh..."

"You haven't looked at it yet?"

The disappointment dripped in her voice, and it weighed him down. He felt bad for taking his time and not making her car a priority. He should have started on it this morning instead of messing around at the coffee shop. Instead of coming to the bed and breakfast for the sole purpose of talking to Ethan about the shop. He could have given Ethan a call and had an answer within a minute or two. Now, almost three hours later, Carter had to explain why her car was sitting unattended in his shop and why he was sitting there instead.

"I know you're wanting your car fixed as soon as possible," Carter said, wishing he'd been more wise in his decisions.

"But..." Hannah said, leading him to say what he wasn't willing to say.

"But..." he glanced at Ethan, who raised his hands in front of him and slowly backed away from the counter. He mouthed something about running some-where and getting something before he and Catie left the kitchen together.

They had left him alone in the kitchen with Hannah. No one around to protect him from the daggers she was tossing at him as she tried to figure out why her car hadn't been looked at yet. He understood her frustration. He couldn't blame her for being frustrated with the whole situation. But the first thing Carter had to cross off his list was Vince's SUV.

"I can't get to your car until the end of this week," he said, wanting to run out of the kitchen and take cover.

"What? Why?" Hannah's questions were filled with worry, and he tried his best to calm her fears. "I know I promised that I would start on it right away, but I forgot that I had Vince's vehicle and a few others right behind it at the garage."

Hannah slowly nodded, and if he weren't mistaken, he could have sworn there were tears brimming in her eyes. The last thing he wanted was to cause her more stress. He didn't want to see her cry either.

"I'm sorry," he said sincerely. He meant it. It was an honest mistake on his part, and not a way he liked to handle business.

"What would I have to pay you to get my car done earlier?"

Carter almost choked on his coffee as he focused on what she had asked. There was no amount of money that could move her car to the front of the line. Considering the front of the line was currently occupied by a law enforcement vehicle. Law enforcement trumped all others in the garage.

"Vince is the deputy here in Maple Glen," Carter explained, keeping his voice low and sincere. "His vehicle has been quite a pain in the neck to figure out, but I'm confident I can have it finished by mid-week."

Hannah blew out a frustrated sigh, and he could only hope that she wasn't too upset with him. It wasn't like she didn't have a warm place to stay or anything to eat. Catie's bed and breakfast was the perfect place to house a woman and her child while waiting for their car to be fixed.

"So you're sure that my car will be ready by the end of the week?"

He nodded, feeling less confident about it than he had a few moments ago.

"Okay," she finally said after several seconds of silence ticked by.

"Okay?"

She nodded. He was more than thankful that she was okay with having to wait. He thought about the ice fishing trip he wanted to take, but quickly dismissed it. He needed to stick around Maple Glen and stay focused on the job.

"But," she said, leaning forward and resting her elbows on the counter. He quirked a brow, wondering what she was going to say next. "I need to know what's wrong with it and how much it's going to cost before you fix it, okay?"

Carter nodded once again. That was part of running the business. He never started working on a vehicle without first consulting with the owner. It was shady business to do such a thing—nickel and diming a customer. That was something he would never do— no matter how hard up for money he was.

"Deal." He grabbed his truck keys and stood up. "You have my word."

A smile spread across Hannah's face.

If there was one thing Carter knew, it was that he would rather see a thousand smiles on Hannah's face than one single tear.

Chapter Seven

HANNAH WATCHED CARTER WALK OUT THE front door as she stood next to Catie while holding a happy-go-lucky baby in her arms. She didn't like having to wait for her car to get fixed. But she hated the fact that her sister had put her in this crummy situation in the first place.

If Ashley had paid the rent on time, along with several other bills, Hannah would still have a place to call home. *Home.*

The word itself had once meant something to Hannah. It had once meant a place to gather and share joy with loved ones while making memories, at least in her dreams. Now she was homeless and left without the possibility of making memories worth sharing with her sister down the road.

Catie's voice pulled her from her thoughts as she reached out for Grace. Hannah gladly accepted Catie's offer to take her for a few minutes. She chastised herself for allowing self-pity to get the best of her. Wallowing in self-pity wasn't going to do her, or Grace, any good and neither would dwelling on the past. She needed to realize that she could only do one thing at a time, and right now, that was to wait for her car to get fixed.

"Ethan and I have been talking about having our own little family one day," Catie said with a wide smile on her face. Hannah feigned a smile of her own, pretending she knew exactly what that felt like—to want a family and be able to have one. "But I told him first things first."

Hannah raised a brow and asked, "Which is?"

Catie turned her attention away from Grace while she wiggled her ring finger in front of her. Hannah knew exactly what she was expecting from Ethan before Catie said, "First comes love, then comes marriage, then—"

"Comes a baby in the baby carriage," Hannah sang out with a wide smile. She recalled singing that loud and proud at recess time while attending elementary school. The boys would run for cover and tease the girls about having cooties before they admitted how cute they thought the girls were.

The thought made Hannah chuckle.

"It's crazy how those silly songs stick with us, right?" Catie asked, now walking toward the couch and motioning for Hannah to sit down next to her.

"Anyway," she said not even a second later, changing the subject, "what'd my brother have to say? I'm sorry I left you alone with him. I hope he wasn't rude."

Hannah smiled and waved off Catie's apology. She had wondered why Catie and Ethan had left the two of them alone, but it hadn't bothered her really. "Not at all," Hannah said, thinking about their conversation. It had been short and sweet, but there was something about the way he looked at her—like he was trying to read through her and figure her out. "He just mentioned that it was going to take a bit longer than he'd expected before he could get my car fixed."

Catie nodded and rolled her eyes. Hannah wouldn't ask what that expression was all about. She didn't care as long as her car was fixed and returned to her by the end of the week as Carter had promised.

"Well, if there's one thing I know for certain about my brother," Catie said as she rocked little Grace in her arms, "It's that he doesn't make a promise if he's not plannin' on keeping it."

Hannah nodded and felt reassured by Catie's words. She didn't like to think of people in a negative light, but she wouldn't deny that she'd had a fear that her car would be put off until whenever. She knew better than to pass judgement without the facts first, but she'd been let down too many times in the last year that she wasn't trusting anything or anyone.

Except Carter. He was the exception because there was just something about him. She wasn't quite sure what it was, but it was definitely something worth noting and paying attention to.

"Do you have a lot of family back in Chicago?" Catie asked as she handed Grace back to Hannah.

Hannah's heart beat against her chest as her brain wildly screamed for her not to answer the question. There was no way around it. She needed to come up with something. Anything. Catie looked over at her, focusing her eyes on Hannah's face. Hannah wondered if the woman could see the beads of sweat forming on her forehead. She focused on slowing her breathing and finding something to say. A lie. Even a little one was something Hannah refused to tell. But the truth wasn't something she was ready for people to know.

"Yeah," she finally spit out. The word left her mouth in a whoosh as the air escaped her lungs. She took a slow, deep breath and tried to focus. "I have a sister."

Catie smiled. And without taking much notice of Hannah's anxiety spiking through the roof, Catie said, "Sisters are the best, aren't they? I have two sisters that I love to death."

Hannah faked another smile, trying her best to keep it together. She hated talking about her family. She didn't have much to talk about when it came to the Michaelson family. Her grandparents had long since passed away, along with both of her parents. She had Ashley as a sister, but that was neither here nor there.

"I know you've met my sister, Cassie, but have you had a chance to meet Cara?" Catie's question was filled with excitement. There was no doubt that she loved her sisters as much as a sister should. Hannah shook her head with yet another forced smile.

She felt sick to her stomach at the mention of family. Sisters. Her thoughts raced with what Ashley had done. Where Ashley could possibly be. What her sister was currently doing instead of what she should have been doing. Ashley *should* have been at home taking care of Grace. She should have been figuring out what to make for lunch and preparing it right about now.

"Cara has a little girl, too. Maybe later I can take you to the coffee shop and have you meet her," Catie said. She glanced at the clock on the wall above the fireplace mantel and stood up from the couch. "Are you hungry? I think I'm going to make us somethin' to eat for lunch."

Hannah was going to deny being hungry until her stomach growled at the mention of food. She would have grabbed a couple of the leftover pancakes, had Carter not taken them all for himself. She shrugged with a kind smile. "Sure," she said, standing with a stretch and placing Grace on her right hip. "I'm going to head upstairs and change little miss here and grab her a bottle."

Catie nodded as she turned and headed for the kitchen. "I'll see you in a few minutes, then," she called out over her shoulder and disappeared into the kitchen.

Hannah looked at Grace who was gnawing on her toy keys locked tightly in her tiny fist. "This is going to take some getting used to, Gracie."

Grace cooed and continued on with the toy in her mouth as Hannah carried her up the steps. She wondered what on earth she was going to do about formula and diapers. She didn't have a lot of money left in her purse. Not after filling the car with a full tank of gas and buying what she needed for Grace in the first place—a winter coat, hat, and mittens.

Her heart sped up at the thought of running out of money before she even left Maple Glen. Her car bill would be enough to break her, especially after adding in the late-night service charge for towing.

She took a deep breath and walked down the hall-way. She needed to focus on taking things one day at a time. There was no sense in getting worked up over something out of her control.

But then again, she would run out of money and then what? She'd be homeless, carless, and stuck in Maple Glen.

Hannah cringed at the thought. She couldn't chance not making it to Tara's. At least at Tara's, she would be with her best friend without the worry of judgement. Her best friend already knew everything there was to know about Hannah and her life. There wasn't much hidden from Tara that she was currently hiding from the Mitchell family at the moment.

What would they think about Hannah if the truth came out?

She couldn't think about that right now. She could only take one day at a time and do the best she could with what she had. If it came time for the truth to come out about being homeless and being dealt a bad hand at the age of twenty-three, so be it.

Most twenty-three-year-olds she'd known were engaged and working in successful careers. Unlike Hannah, they were working toward making their dreams come true with each passing day—one step closer than the day before. Hannah wasn't even sure what it was like to have a clear vision of what a positive future looked like.

"Enough of the negative thoughts," she chastised herself out loud, setting Grace down in the crib before making her way over to her unpacked bags.

Hannah glanced around the room. She took in how neat and clean it was. Not one thing had been out of place since she'd arrived. She smiled at the framed pictures hanging on the wall. One stood out to her from across the room, causing her to take a few steps in that direction to get a better look.

The familiar painting stared back at her as she traced a finger along the edge of the frame. Her grandmother once had the same exact painting hanging above the mantel in her living room. The painting was the center of attention in her grandmother's house as it continuously pulled wandering eyes to it.

Hannah smiled at the memories that the painting evoked. She loved her grandmother more than life itself. Her grandmother had allowed Hannah and Ashley to stay several days and nights while their parents were at home drinking without a care in the world.

Her grandmother's words still stuck with Hannah after all these years later. "You are not to blame for what others choose to do with their life. You are only responsible for how you live yours and how you choose to handle the cards you've been dealt."

Tears stung the back of Hannah's eyes as she recalled the night she'd been sitting next to her grandmother on her seventies-style couch with bright orange and yellow flowers mixed with only who knows what other patterns. Hannah and Ashley had been picked up by their grandfather that night after their parents had a fight. It wasn't anything Hannah and Ashley hadn't already heard or witnessed before, but their grandparents insisted on picking them up when Ashley called them crying.

Hannah swiped away a stray tear and shook her head. For all the times she and Ashley had tried to blame themselves for their parents' worries and arguments, their grandparents had been there for them while assuring them they had nothing to worry about. That everything was going to be alright.

A soft knock sounded behind Hannah. She quickly wiped away the stray tears that streamed down her cheeks and pulled herself together before turning around.

She had expected to see Catie standing in the doorway, but instead, it was Carter.

"Oh... gosh... I... Um..."

He held up a hand to stop her from struggling, and she couldn't thank him enough for that. It was more than embarrassing to have him stand there and witness the mess she was with tears streaming down her face. "I'm sorry. I should've maybe called instead, but I—"

"It's okay," she said, waving off his apology. She dabbed at her cheeks with the sleeve of her sweatshirt and shook her head. "It's not your fault I'm a mess. I guess everything's just piling up and I'm thinking about what I'm going to do when my car's actually fixed, and I'm—"

"Hey," he said, stepping into the room and offering her a sympathetic smile. "It's okay. I'm not sure what's going on, but I can assure you that I've been through enough in my lifetime to know that everything works out in the end."

She smiled through the tears, and for once felt a sense of comfort. "Thanks."

She watched as his lips curved into a half smile. "Anytime," he said with a wink. "But wait," he said with his hands raised in front of him, "there's more."

She raised a brow, trying to figure out what on earth was going on.

"I took a look at your car as soon as I got back to the shop, and I think I just figured out what's wrong with your car... and like I promised, I'm letting you know before I order the part," he said, a proud look on his face as he waited for her to react to what he'd just told her. "It's the alternator, and I can have one here within a day or two. Once the part is here, I'll be able to start workin' on it. You'll be back on the road in no time at all."

Hannah felt the weight on her shoulders lift as she gave him the okay to order the part. In that moment, she realized that Carter might be right. Everything would be okay. She just needed to give it time.

Chapter Eight

CARTER DIDN'T SEE HIMSELF AS AN emotional kind of guy, but then again, he was never face to face with a woman who was breaking down in front of him. If only he would have just called her instead of coming to the bed and breakfast with the good news, he would not have to see the tears welling in her soft brown eyes.

He was far from being emotional, but that didn't mean he didn't have a heart. He could tell by the way she worried her teeth over her bottom lip that she was far from okay.

"What do you say we go get some coffee at Fran's?" he blurted out, realizing that he'd been standing in the room and staring at her for the last ten minutes without saying a word. She had busied herself with looking after Grace—doing the nurturing things a mother would do with a baby—as he stood there silently watching and taking in the beauty of the room. "I mean... not as a date or anything. I just thought since my sister hasn't followed through with her word of taking you there, I might as well be the one."

He silently chided himself for allowing the words to fall out of his mouth without rhyme or reason. He sounded like a rambling idiot, and if she turned down his offer, he wouldn't blame her.

"Catie's cooking lunch," Hannah said, snapping the baby's clothes in place after changing a dirty diaper. He watched in awe as he held his breath. That's one thing he was in no hurry for—babies and their dirty diapers.

He felt the urge to say 'so what,' but then he thought of making his sister cook for nothing. It wouldn't be fair to Catie just because he wanted to take Hannah and Grace to meet Fran.

"Okay," he said, accepting her answer and assuming it would still be no tomorrow and the day after that, too. He ran a hand through his hair and scratched the back of his neck. "I guess I'll just head to the shop and get back to work. I'll get that part ordered so I have it ready when I finish with the other cars I'm working on."

He tried not to let the sound of disappointment weigh too heavily in his voice, but he had no control over it once the words were out of his mouth. He needed to work on the effect Hannah had on him when she was around if he didn't want to continue making a fool of himself.

"That's probably a good idea," she said with a teasing smile as she lifted Grace up off of the bed. "I plan on leaving Maple Glen sometime soon."

For some reason or another, he had allowed himself to forget, if only for a minute, that she was leaving. He wasn't sure why it mattered so much to him, or why he even cared to strike up a friendship with her. She was a stranger in his hometown and, more importantly, she more than likely had something going on in her life that she didn't want anyone to know—including him.

But then again, he was good at reading people. And the fact of the matter was, at the end of the day, he was intrigued by Hannah and he found himself wanting to know more about her. Not because he wanted to fall in love and all of that overrated, mushy stuff, but for the simple reason of having someone to talk to. Someone who was troubled like him and could relate to him.

It didn't take a genius to figure out that Hannah was close to his age. If not the same age, he was only off a year or two—give or take.

The thought of the *L* word crossed his mind one last time as he took a step toward the bedroom door. He hated to even think of it, let alone believe in it. Why did he want to take her to Fran's, then?

Fran was Maple Glen's queen of matchmaking.

Taking Hannah to meet Fran would be setting her up for an ambush. Especially with his sisters and soon-to-be sisters.

He shook his head and cleared the thoughts.

"I'll see ya later," he said and stepped out of the bedroom.

"How about tomorrow instead?"

Hannah's question caught him by surprise. He stepped back and peeked his head around the door-frame. "Tomorrow?"

His heart galloped in his chest at the thought of taking her with him. At the thought that she was agreeing to go with him in the first place. Maybe he wasn't such a loner after all.

"Yes." She smiled and said, "Unless you have cars to work on or something more important to do?"

He caught her teasing grin and shook his head. He was going to have to get used to having a witty remark at the ready from now on. Hannah was full of it. And he liked that.

"I have plenty of cars to work on," Carter said with a grin. "But they can wait until after I have coffee with you and little Grace there."

He pointed at the baby and smiled. He was young, but he wasn't dumb. Carter knew that he needed to include the baby. He'd been raised a gentleman, and a gentleman he'd always be.

~

CARTER STILL WASN'T SURE WHAT HE HAD been thinking when he invited her to Aunt Fran's coffee shop the day before. In all honesty, he was just being nice and didn't see any sense in having Hannah stay inside the bed and breakfast all day, every day.

It wouldn't hurt for her to go out and take a tour of the town. Carter had no problem with showing her what Maple Glen was all about. He loved the town, and he couldn't find one reason a person like Hannah wouldn't like it.

He hopped into his truck and turned the key, praying the old truck wouldn't let him down. One day, he would buy himself a brand new truck and retire the old one for odd jobs here and there around town—like hauling things to the landfill or helping Miss Betty's niece move her things from one place to another.

But he couldn't afford to buy a new truck just yet. Business was slower than he'd like, and things were a bit worrisome. Nothing worth panicking about, but it was still something he needed to keep an eye on. Winter months were always harder than most.

Aside from that, things were good in Maple Glen.

He pulled into the drive leading to the bed and breakfast and shifted into park. He left the truck running in an attempt to keep it warm as he walked up the porch steps.

Carter opened the screen door and rapped his knuckles on the solid oak door. Duke's loud bark was followed by a low and steady growl from somewhere on the other side of the door. Carter found a sense of relief to know that his sister was well protected by the black lab. He'd feel sorry for the person who decided to break into the bed and breakfast.

Not that break-ins were common in their small town. There was never anything more than the occasional bingo parlor call or an occasional parking ticket —as his sister Cara should know.

The door opened, and the smell of bacon greeted him before Catie could invite him in. "You know the door is always open," she said, leading him into the living room and motioning for him to take a seat.

He hitched a thumb over his shoulder and said, "I'm only here for a minute. I left the truck runnin' and I figured—"

"Hannah," Catie called out, walking over to the bottom of the stairs. "Your date's here."

Carter felt his face redden. It had been a while since his sister was able to embarrass him, and by the look on her face, she was enjoying herself. "It's not a date," he whispered with a furrowed brow. "Cut it out."

Catie offered a subtle shrug and a wink before scurrying off into the kitchen. Within a minute, Catie popped back out and said, "You know Fran's going to love this."

Carter shot her a glare just as he heard footsteps coming from upstairs. He moved to the bottom of the staircase to wait for her. "Good mornin'."

"Morning," she said with a shy smile. She carried

Grace close to her chest, as any good mother would, while descending the stairs. He watched as she carefully took each step, making sure to be there in case she tripped. "Let me grab a clean bottle for Grace from the kitchen, and then we'll be ready to go."

He could hear Catie and Hannah whispering back and forth in the kitchen, and even though he kept his feet planted in one spot, he was still curious as to what the two of them were talking about.

Hannah emerged from the kitchen with Grace on one hip and a diaper bag on the other. She smiled as she walked toward him. "I think we're ready," she said, pulling Grace's stocking hat down over her ears and kissing her button nose. Carter watched in awe at the love of a mother.

"Alright, then, let's go get some coffee," he said, grabbing the car seat from the bench sitting by the front door and motioning for Hannah to go on ahead of him. He walked out of the house behind them, carefully watching to make sure she didn't slip.

He went ahead of Hannah and Grace and opened the passenger side door before placing the car seat in first. He wasn't quite sure how the thing was supposed to go, so he offered to hold Grace while allowing Hannah to fasten it into the front seat of his truck.

When she climbed out, she took Grace from his arms and smiled. "Thanks."

Carter patiently waited while Hannah buckled

Grace into the car seat. "We're ready," Hannah said after she buckled herself in.

He nodded with a smile as he closed the door for Hannah before making his way over to his side and climbing in the driver's seat. He smiled down at the baby sitting next to him in the front seat between him and Hannah. He wasn't used to having a baby riding along with him, but one could say that he could get used to it.

Carter shifted the truck into drive and followed the driveway roundabout onto the road. The thought of Fran crossed his mind, but he wasn't worried about it. Everyone liked Fran, and he didn't doubt for one second that Hannah would like her, too.

Chapter Nine

"THIS IS KIND OF AWKWARD, ISN'T IT?"

Carter's question broke through the silence in the cab of his truck. Hannah had been too focused on her own thoughts about what to expect at the coffee shop to realize the two of them hadn't said a word since leaving the bed and breakfast's driveway.

"Awkward?" she asked, raising a brow in Carter's direction. He seemed uptight and uncertain as he held tightly to the steering wheel, causing his knuckles to whiten. She wondered if maybe he was regretting his offer to take her out for coffee. "How so?"

He shrugged his broad shoulders and flashed her a nervous smile. "You don't think it's awkward that the mechanic who's supposed to be fixin' your car is takin' you to the coffee shop?"

She smiled and shook her head. "Nope."

She had experienced several awkward situations in her lifetime, but she wouldn't add having a man invite her along for a cup of coffee to the list. She could feel his eyes on her, studying her and trying to figure her out. Maybe he was used to women not telling him the truth. Or maybe she was looking too far into what his eyes were telling her.

"You should watch the road," she stated, keeping her eyes on the road and hoping he'd do the same. She rested an arm across Grace in the car seat. A subtle precaution just in case Carter's staring caused an accident.

"I know these roads like the back of my hand," he said confidently. She fought back the urge to roll her eyes, knowing well enough that accidents could happen in a matter of seconds.

"Even the most confident drivers can have accidents," she said with a pointed tone. "Or cause them."

Out of the corner of her eye she watched Carter turn his attention back on the road. She released the breath she'd been holding and relaxed into the seat. She wasn't afraid of much in life, other than the obvious things, but now that she had Grace to take care of...

"I do have to warn you, though," Carter said, keeping his eyes on the road as he talked, "my aunt Fran has the best coffee in town, but she also has a reputation."

Hannah recalled the warning she'd already been

given about Fran. The banter between Grant and Cassie had quickly evolved to include what happens when Fran gets involved. Hannah hadn't been too sure about what it meant, and still she had no clue. "Reputation?"

Carter nodded with a grin. "Rumor has it that she's the town's queen of matchmaking."

Hannah slowly caught on to what he was saying. She had watched plenty of romance movies on Hallmark and Lifetime to know just what kind of matchmaking Carter was talking about.

"I see."

"She's been successful with my brothers and sisters, ya know?"

Hannah wasn't liking where this was going. If Carter knew that his aunt would enjoy playing matchmaker, why would he think bringing Hannah with him was a good idea?

"What about you?" she asked, silently slapping herself for asking such a stupid question. What about him? It wasn't like she actually cared to know.

"She hasn't caught me yet," Carter said with a smirk. He sure was confident in his ways. Hannah had noticed that right away. From the very first night he had come to her rescue, she could tell that he was a man of confidence and few words.

"Yet."

Hannah's voice cracked at the realization of what awaited her. If Fran thought for one minute that she was going to place a target on Hannah... She couldn't allow that to happen. Not now. Not ever.

Carter cleared his throat, causing Hannah to snap out of her thoughts. She didn't need Cupid shooting arrows in her direction while she was trying to get out of there. She didn't want love or anything like it to find her. As soon as her car was fixed, she was gone.

The small coffee shop came into view, sitting across from what appeared to be his family's meat locker and deli.

"Here we are," Carter confirmed as he guided the truck into an empty parking spot out front.

Hannah didn't want to appear nervous. She wanted to appear as confident as Carter when she walked into the coffee shop. Taking a deep breath, she glanced at Carter and released it slowly. She didn't know what she had been thinking when she accepted his invitation for coffee. She could only hope it didn't involve anything more than an iced frappuccino.

"WELL, WHO DO WE HAVE HERE?" AN OLDER woman asked, making her way around the counter toward them. Hannah froze with Grace in her arms. She might have thought she was ready to meet people in Maple Glen, but she might have thought wrong.

"This must be Hannah?" the woman asked, reaching out and wrapping Hannah in a hug. Grace squirmed in her arms, more than likely sensing the unease Hannah felt with the woman's embrace. The woman took a step back and turned her attention to the baby in Hannah's arms. "And this must be Grace?"

Carter stepped forward and rested an arm on the woman's shoulders. "Aunt Fran, this is Hannah and her little girl, Grace."

Hannah bit the inside of her lip as he introduced them, hoping that Fran wouldn't call her bluff. It was hard to pull off being a mother. It wasn't for the faint of heart, but someone had to do it. And in this case, it was Hannah.

"It's so nice to meet you," Fran said, taking another step back and allowing Hannah the ability to breathe again. "I bet it was scary being stranded out in the middle of nowhere."

Hannah nodded, not wanting to remember how it felt to be all alone on the side of the road with a baby in the backseat.

"I'm just glad the Mitchell kids were able to help you," she said with a wide, proud smile, and Hannah nodded. "Me, too."

"Well, that's enough chitter chatterin'," Fran said, slapping her hands against her thighs. "Let's get ya somethin' to drink. Follow me."

The pep in Fran's step didn't go unnoticed. Hannah enjoyed the enthusiasm that radiated from Fran. There was nothing like having an upbeat start to a person's morning.

"What can I get ya?" Fran asked, looking straight at Hannah. Hannah turned toward Carter, but Fran said, "I already know what he's havin'. He always has the same thing anyhow."

Hannah smiled when Carter looked at her with a telling smile. "It's true. I'm a man of habit."

"I'll just have an iced caramel frappuccino, please," Hannah said, looking up at the board hanging behind Fran.

"Comin' right up. You guys can go and take a seat. I'll bring it over when it's ready," Fran said, motioning them toward a booth in the corner of the coffee shop.

Hannah allowed Carter to lead the way, but noticed he seemed to duck and hide from a booth full of women who were laughing over coffee.

She slid into the booth across from him, shifting Grace to her other arm while studying Carter. He didn't say anything, but that didn't mean a thing. She'd just witnessed him dodging into a booth like shots had been fired at him.

"Who are they?" Hannah asked, pointing over his shoulder. He reached out and gently pressed her hand down. "Don't point. You'll get their attention."

Hannah quirked a brow and wondered what on earth Carter was trying to hide from. "You don't want them to see me with you?"

Carter shrugged and softened his expression. "Somethin' like that."

Hannah slowly nodded, coming to terms with what wasn't being said. "I see."

Before she had a chance to ask him anything else, Fran was setting their drinks down in front of them and sliding into the booth next to Carter. "I hope you don't mind if I sit for a minute. I've been on my feet all mornin', and I just need a quick break," she said, fanning her face regardless of the fact that it wasn't close to being too hot in the shop. There was actually a slight chill in the air since they were sitting so close to the large, frost-covered window. Not to mention the outside temperature couldn't have been above thirty degrees with more snow on the way.

"She's so cute," Fran said, motioning toward Grace, who was now dozing off in Hannah's arms. "How old is she?"

"She just turned six months last week," Hannah said with a smile.

Fran's eyes beamed with elation while looking at Grace. Hannah knew it wasn't uncommon for older women to fuss over babies, so she allowed herself to relax a bit more and let her guard down as she settled into the booth.

"So, Hannah," Fran said, "has Carter shown you around town yet?"

Hannah looked at Carter for the answer even though she knew it. He offered a subtle shrug and said, "Not yet, Aunt Fran. She hasn't been in town *that* long. I figured I'd let her settle in before I take her on a guided tour."

Hannah smiled at the sarcasm she heard in Carter's voice.

Fran slapped at him and said, "You don't have to get smart with me. I was just makin' conversation, is all."

Carter nodded and quickly apologized to Fran.

"Anywho," Fran said, focusing back on Hannah. Hannah couldn't help but smile. So far, she liked Fran. She reminded her of a woman she had known when she was a child. She'd met her at the nursing home where her grandmother stayed after Alzheimer's took a toll on her. "I've heard that you're from Chicago?"

Hannah nodded, stealing a quick glance at Carter. "Yes, born and raised there."

"What brings you so far from home?"

Home. The word stood out like a sore thumb. Hannah didn't have a place to call home, but she wasn't going to tell Fran that. Instead, she said, "Just taking some time off from work to visit an old friend."

"Plenty of time before the holiday rush, I suppose," Fran said with another wide smile. They had only just met, but there was something about Fran that made Hannah feel like she'd known her her whole life—aside from the similarities of Miss Jenkins at the nursing home.

"Well, I suppose I should let you two have some quiet time together," Fran said, sliding to the edge of the booth and standing with a stretch. "Don't let Carter here fool ya. He's got the kindest heart you'll ever find here in Maple Glen."

Fran gave Hannah a wink and walked away. Hannah was taken aback by her statement, wondering why on earth the woman had said it in the first place.

"It's okay. She's random like that," Carter explained with a light chuckle. "If I didn't know her antics so well, I'd think she was losing her mind."

Hannah reached for her drink and slid it closer. Grace was getting heavy in her arms, but she hadn't thought to bring the car seat inside with them. She took a sip from the straw and melted into the booth. "That's amazing."

"Thank you," Fran called out from the same booth Carter had tried to avoid. Hannah smiled and shifted Grace around in her arms once again in an attempt to keep them from falling asleep.

"Would you like me to hold her for a bit?"

The sincerity in Carter's voice made Hannah's heart skip a beat. The question alone had caused her to swoon, but the way he looked at her with those soft brown eyes...

"Here," he said, reaching out for Grace without giving Hannah a chance to say no. She accepted his offer by handing her niece over to him, making sure that he had a good hold on Grace before letting go. "I—"

"Aww," the group of women Carter had been trying to avoid sang out in unison.

Hannah glanced at Carter, who shook his head and tried to tell her just to ignore them, but ignoring them was easier said than done. The women at the table, including Fran, were all watching Carter with wide grins on their faces. One of the women at the table had a little girl in her arms.

As soon as Hannah made eye contact with the woman and the child, the woman smiled and stood from her spot at the table. Hannah held her breath as the woman approached their booth, hoping she wouldn't ask motherly questions that only an actual mother could possibly know.

"You must be Hannah, right?"

Hannah forced a smile and said, "Yep. And this is Grace. We're the ones who were stranded right outside of town."

The woman nodded and shifted the little one to her other side before offering a hand in Hannah's direction. "I'm Cara," she said, "Carter's sister."

Hannah accepted her hand and smiled. Catie had mentioned Cara. It was good to put a face with a name. She looked at the little girl who was resting her head on Cara's shoulder.

"This is my daughter, Ellie," Cara said, kissing the side of her daughter's face. Hannah watched the interaction between mother and daughter. Watching the two of them made it even more obvious that Hannah and Grace were not mother and daughter. In no way, shape, or form. In no time at all people would start suspecting something wasn't right about Hannah and Grace. It would only be a matter of time before people started asking questions.

"How old is your little girl?" Cara asked, pointing at Grace who was asleep in Carter's arms. He didn't seem to mind, though. Hannah tried to keep her swooning heart under control as she said, "She's six months old."

Cara looked over her shoulder and turned back to Hannah. "It was nice meeting you. I hope you enjoy your stay at the bed and breakfast while you're in town."

"Of course," Hannah said. "I couldn't ask for a better place to be while getting my car fixed."

Cara glanced down at Carter and back to Hannah. She hitched a thumb in Carter's direction and whispered, "Let's hope he doesn't take as long fixin' yours as he did mine."

Carter shook his head and shooed his sister away. "Get out of here," he said in a hushed voice, quiet enough not to wake the baby in his arms.

Cara offered one last 'nice to meet you' and walked away. Hannah watched as Cara took her spot back and said something to the others at the table. They turned and looked at Hannah with friendly smiles lining their lips. Hannah waved, feeling a bit more at ease with her surroundings.

Carter's family seemed down to earth and easy to get along with.

"They're sayin' the snow will be here within the next hour or so," Fran said, making her way over to Hannah and Carter. "You two should get little Grace back home where it's warm."

"I've heard the storm's supposed to drop about two feet of snow," Fran said. She looked at Hannah and added, "If the storm's as bad as the weatherman's sayin', you might be stayin' in Maple Glen a lot longer than planned."

Hannah slid to the edge of the booth and shrugged into her coat. She didn't want to hear about the weather or what the chances of her staying in the small town were because of it.

She reached for Grace, but Carter shook his head and said, "I've got her. Go on ahead. I'll follow you out."

Hannah grabbed the diaper bag, along with her purse, and turned toward Fran. "Thank you for the coffee. It was nice meeting you."

Fran's face lit up with a smile. "It's my pleasure, dear. Take care."

Hannah offered a quick wave goodbye to the women in the booth and headed for the door. She glanced over her shoulder to make sure that Carter was behind her. Her heart skipped a beat at the sight of him wrapping Grace in his arms, pulling her close to his chest, and draping his coat around her in an effort to protect her from the cold they were about to endure.

Hannah smiled and allowed her heart to soften toward the rugged mechanic who seemed too confident and cocky for his own good. It hadn't taken long for the softer side of Carter Mitchell to shine through —just like his aunt Fran had told her it would.

Chapter Ten

CARRYING THE BABY IN HIS ARMS AND allowing her to snuggle close to his chest opened up a can of worms he'd rather not think about at the moment. He needed to focus on getting the girls into his truck and back to the bed and breakfast before the snowstorm hit.

He wasn't afraid of snow, but it wasn't about him. He wanted to make sure Hannah and Grace were taken care of and settled in somewhere warm. The bed and breakfast was the perfect place, exactly as Cara had said. It was just one more thing to be proud of when it came to his family.

"I'm not sure the storm's going to be as bad as they say," Carter said, shifting the truck into drive and pulling away from the coffee shop. He cranked the heat up and scrubbed at the inside of his window. It hadn't taken long for the windows to frost over.

When Hannah didn't say anything, he looked at her. She was sitting as silent as could be while watching the snowflakes fall against the windshield of his pickup. He'd seen the worried expression cross her face when his aunt had mentioned the snow. He knew that she wasn't planning to stay in Maple Glen. And he also knew that she wouldn't still be there if it hadn't been for her car breaking down.

"Have you talked to your friend, Tina?"

"Tara?"

"Yeah." He had never been too good with remembering names—except for one. He smiled at her. "Sorry. Do I get partial credit for gettin' the *T* right?"

She laughed at that, allowing him to relax just a bit.

"So... have you?"

"I texted her and told her that I wouldn't be there for at least another day or so," Hannah said. She was still looking straight ahead.

"Well, that's good. At least she knows where you're at and that you're okay," he said, trying to lighten the mood hanging heavily between them. He wondered why Hannah never said more than a few words about her hometown or her friend. He also wondered if there was something more to it that she wasn't telling him. "Besides your friend that you're going to see, do you have any family back home?"

Hannah flashed him a look, and in that split second, there was proof of something left unsaid. He didn't want to push it, but he couldn't deny the fact that curiosity was getting the best of him. Especially now that he couldn't just walk away and be okay with it. He was invested.

"Why do you ask?"

Her question was straight and to the point, but it wasn't what he expected her to say. Most people took the time to talk about their families. Their friends. Heck, he would have even loved to hear about her job and what she did for a living in that big city of hers.

Instead, he offered a subtle shrug and turned his attention back on the road ahead of them. "Just curious. That's all."

Hannah released a sigh, and he thought maybe she was going to tell him something he wanted to hear. Something that would tell him more about her. Not just about where she came from as far as the city lines went, but more about her family, her dreams, and what she wanted in her future... in Grace's future. More important than that... if she had a man back home.

"I have a sister," she said in a soft whisper. If he hadn't been paying attention, he wouldn't have heard her. "It's just her and me. Or... *was*, anyway."

The sadness in her voice caused him to pay closer attention. He hadn't wanted to cause hard feelings or rough emotions. He felt foolish for even pressing the issue, especially since it wasn't any of his business.

"She has a lot of problems going on that I can't help her with," Hannah explained, taking a deep breath in and releasing it slowly. He wanted to reach out and touch her. Tell her that whatever was going on, it wouldn't last forever. Nothing bad ever lasted forever. Just the same as the good.

Instead, he held tightly to the steering wheel and resisted the urge. He guided the truck along the back roads that lead them to the bed and breakfast.

"Sometimes we can't help the ones we love, because they have to help themselves first," he said, unsure if he'd said the right thing. But it only made sense that he say it because it was true and he had a feeling she needed to hear it. It was obvious that she was carrying a burden that wasn't hers to carry.

"I don't think that's going to happen anytime soon," Hannah said as she glanced over at him. He pulled the truck into the driveway and shifted into park. Instead of turning the truck off, he left it running. He didn't want to end their time together. Especially not now that he was getting her to open up to him. "Ashley doesn't see it the way I see it. She never has, and probably never will."

Carter knew what it was like having siblings that disagreed with the way he saw things. It happened more times than he'd like to admit, but that's what made his family stronger. The bond they shared didn't come from everything being a nice, easy walk in the park on a summer day. They'd had their share of arguments and backyard fights. Fights that involved tossing the boxing gloves and bloodying their knuckles.

But they grew up and matured with time—Carter

being the last of the seven. Looking back, Carter wouldn't change a single thing about the way he'd been raised or how he and his siblings got along.

"Does she know that you're here?" Carter wasn't one to pry in a person's business, but he couldn't resist the need to know more about Hannah. He could have dropped her and Grace off and left. Called it a day. But like a magnet, she was pulling him in and he couldn't leave.

Hannah combed her fingers through her hair, an attempt to hide the fact that she was crying. "I'm sorry," he said as he reached over and touched her hand. "I didn't mean to—"

"It's okay," Hannah said. He thought about pulling his hand back, but she allowed his hand to stay resting on top of hers. "My life just isn't the greatest right now."

"If it makes you feel any better, my life isn't the greatest either."

Hannah turned and looked at him. Maybe she thought he was just saying it, making it up to make her feel better about the life she was obviously battling herself over, but he meant it.

"I know it's hard to believe," he said with a slight grin. "I have trouble believin' it myself."

She cracked a smile and wiped away the stray tears streaming down her cheeks. He smiled knowing that he'd taken her mind away from the one thing that was bothering her—even if only for a minute.

"I'm serious, though," he said, thinking about the troubles he'd had over the last year. "I've been struggling to make ends meet for the last few months, and here my siblings are..."

"Killing it?"

"Yeah, pretty much." Carter chuckled at the ridiculousness of his envy. He'd never been one to be jealous of what others had, but sometimes it snuck up and got the best of him. "I mean... I'm happy for them. Look," he motioned to the house sitting in front of his truck. "Catie's got the house of her dreams, which just so happens to be the same house our grandparents owned since our mother and Aunt Fran were babies. There are a lot of memories in that house."

He wasn't quite sure why he was telling Hannah all about it, but she didn't seem to mind. Instead, she looked at the bed and breakfast in awe and asked, "What about your other siblings? What do they have that you want?"

"Ha. That's a good question," he replied, thinking of what it was exactly that he wanted—that he didn't already have. "I can't really think of anything. I mean... we each have our own business that we're runnin', whether they're in the red or making good money is yet to be determined for some of us... But yeah, I'm not so sure I want anything more than what I've already got."

Hannah nodded along with what he was saying, and he still wanted to know more about her. Was she close to her sister? Were they estranged? Is that why she was headed to her friend's place?

"What about you? Is there anything your sister has that *you* want?"

Hannah let out a soft laugh and tucked a strand of hair behind her ear. "That's a good question," she said, mocking his own response to the very same question she'd asked him to answer. She offered a subtle shrug as she sat next to him. Grace was sound asleep in the car seat next to them and he wondered if that's all babies did—eat, sleep, and sleep some more. "I guess I want the freedom she has. The ability to walk away and not care about who she hurts in the end."

Hannah stopped for a second, just long enough to keep her emotions in check by inhaling a deep breath and releasing it slowly. Carter watched as she regained her composure like a pro—someone who has had to do it numerous times. "The ability to dodge responsibilities and the consequences of not doing what's expected. That's what I'd like. Not to have to worry about everything for once," she said. A painful expression crossed Hannah's face as a tear slid down her cheek. Carter reached up and swiped it away with his thumb. She turned to look at him, a sadness in her eyes and written all over her face that he could have gone without witnessing. She shook her head and gathered her things from the floorboard at her feet. "I'm sorry. I should get inside. I'm sure you have better things to do than listen to my self-pity."

As she reached to unhook Grace's car seat from the front seat, Carter placed his hand on top of hers and met her eyes with his. For one solid minute the world seemed to stand still around them, allowing them the time to see each other for who they might actually be.

"Hannah," he said, slowly forming his thoughts into a sentence, "I'm not sure what happened back home to cause you to leave Chicago, and maybe you don't want me to know and that's perfectly fine, but you're not alone in feeling the way you do. You don't have to apologize for it. We've all felt that way a time or two in our lives. It's okay to feel that way, but you don't have to stay there. Whatever's goin' on can be dealt with and forgotten about."

Hannah's eyes stayed focused on him as she hung to every word he said. He didn't want her to think she was alone, and he didn't want her to think that she needed to apologize for what she thought of as wasting his time.

"Carter, I—" Hannah looked down at Grace and then toward the house. "Thank you," she said. Her words were soft and her eyes full of mixed emotions. He could see the hurricane in her eyes as she battled between staying in the truck and going into the house.

Carter wasn't sure where the conversation left them. He wasn't sure if he'd said something he'd later regret when it would come back and slap him in the face. But there was one thing he was sure of in that very moment. He'd never wanted to care for a woman as much as he did about Hannah.

Hannah. A woman who had been stranded on the side of the road after dark, with a snowstorm on its way. A woman who not only had herself to take care of, but a baby, too. A woman who had so much burden weighing her down, but at the same time, refused to allow anyone the chance to help.

"I better get Grace inside, but thank you for everything today."

She slid away from his hold and opened her door. She grabbed Grace's car seat and hooked her arm through the handle as she lifted it out of the truck.

"Hannah, wait," Carter said, hopping out of the truck and racing to the other side to help her. "Let me carry Grace for you," he offered. He reached out and took the baby in one arm while placing his free hand on Hannah's back as he walked beside her to the front porch steps.

"I enjoyed havin' coffee with you today," Carter said, stopping in front of the screen door and turning toward Hannah. "Maybe we can do it again tomorrow?"

Hannah grinned but shook her head. She reached for Grace and said, "I think it's best if we don't waste any more time. My car needs to be fixed, and my friend's waiting for me to—"

"Okay," he said, handing Grace over and taking a step back.

Carter didn't need to hear another word. He heard her loud and clear. She wanted her car fixed so she could get out of Maple Glen and back to living the life she was trying to run from.

He walked down the steps and turned back to face her. "I'll let you know when I get your car fixed, then. Have a good day."

"Thanks. And you, too," Hannah said as he turned away and walked back to his truck.

He climbed into the driver's seat of his truck and watched as Hannah walked inside without looking back. He wasn't sure what caused her to put the walls back up. Especially since he thought the conversation had done them both some good.

Shaking his head, he backed out of the driveway and headed to the shop. He would get finished with Vince's SUV, something he'd been putting off for a while, and hopefully by tomorrow the part he needed for Hannah's car would be there so he could fix her car and send her and Grace on their merry little way.

Chapter Eleven

THE COFFEE HAD BEEN WONDERFUL, ALONG with her time spent with Carter. She didn't regret going with him to the coffee shop. What she did regret, though, was having a conversation with him. She allowed him a glimpse into what she was holding back, and it scared her.

It scared her even more to know that he understood. To think of the electrical charge that had buzzed through her when he touched her hand. When he wiped the tears from her cheek with his thumb.

"You're back already? I thought you would be gone all day," Catie called out, walking from the kitchen and meeting Hannah by the front entrance. Hannah set Grace's car seat down next to her feet and allowed Catie to take her coat and hang it on one of the coat rack's bronze metal hooks. "How was the coffee?"

"It was amazing," Hannah said, lifting Grace out of the car seat and cradling her in her arms. Catie motioned for Hannah to follow her into the living room and to have a seat on the couch as she sat down in the chair next to it. "I've had plenty of frappuccinos while living in the city, and they're nothing like Fran's."

Catie's eyes lit up. "Did you tell her that? I'm sure it went straight to her head."

They shared a laugh about Fran's confident streak, and Hannah thought about Carter. He had the same confidence that radiated from each member of the Mitchell family she'd met. Pride and confidence was a fair trait shared among them. She wondered how on earth a person went about getting some of their own.

"She's such a hoot, isn't she?" Catie asked, leaning forward and resting her arms on her crossed legs.

"Yes, she is," Hannah replied. Hannah had enjoyed meeting Fran. She seemed to not only be Maple Glen's matchmaker, but also its mother hen. Hannah noticed the way Fran wanted to take care of everyone, and she didn't let a single thing slip through the cracks. "She reminds me of someone I met when I was a child."

Catie held up a finger and said, "Hold that thought. Let me grab us something to drink."

Hannah held the thought until Catie returned to the living room carrying two cups full of sweet tea.

"Thank you," Hannah said, reaching out for hers and setting it down on the table in front of her.

"You're welcome. Sometimes I forget that I'm the hostess of this place," Catie said with a light chuckle, and Hannah laughed along with her. Catie had nothing to worry about when it came to running the bed and breakfast. From the moment Hannah arrived, Catie had been nothing short of pleasant while upholding hospitality like it was her business. "But anyway, back to what you were sayin'," Catie said, taking a drink of her tea and setting the cup back down beside her. "Aunt Fran reminded you of someone from back home?"

"Yeah. When I was younger, my grandma ended up in a nursing home," Hannah explained, recalling memories of what that time had been like for not only her grandmother, but for her and the rest of the family as well. There was truth in the saying that grand-mothers were the glue that held families together. Her family had been the prime example. "But there was this woman who resided there, too. She was actually my grandmother's neighbor for many years before moving into the facility, but I hadn't known that until after my grandmother passed away..."

Hannah inhaled a deep breath before releasing it slowly as she reached for her glass of tea. It had been years since she'd lost her grandmother, but it felt like it had happened yesterday.

"Aunt Fran's a pretty special person," Catie said. "I'm sure some would even say that she's the one the townspeople turn to when they're needing somethin'."

Hannah nodded once again. She could see that. She could also see that being true with the woman from the nursing home before receiving her dementia diagnosis and things had slowly turned for the worse.

Grace stirred in Hannah's arms, and she thought about taking her upstairs and placing her in the crib where she might be more comfortable. It seemed like a good idea. "I'll be right back," Hannah said, standing up and heading toward the staircase leading to their upstairs room. She would lay Grace down in the crib and go back downstairs. Grace would be fine by herself in the crib as she slept, and Hannah would be able to enjoy a couple of hours doing what she wanted.

But before she could do that, she needed to check her phone and see if she had any missed calls or messages.

She was surprised to find several messages waiting for her, but none of them were from the one person she had expected them to be from. Her breath caught in her throat as she glanced at the preview from an unknown number.

She tapped the box and opened the message to read it. Her eyes skimmed the message several times before it sank in. *Carter*. He had sent her a message apologizing for overstepping. He said sorry for asking too many questions and said he hoped she would forgive him and accept his invitation to coffee again in the morning.

She smiled through the stinging of the tears as she

read the message one more time. She had no idea why she'd reacted that way toward him when he dropped them off earlier. It was obvious that he hadn't meant any harm, but deep down, she knew that she couldn't take any chances.

He might have been the sweetest man she'd ever met in her entire life, but she couldn't allow herself to get distracted. Especially not by Carter. She had more things to worry about than just herself, and she didn't need to end up investing her time and heart into something that wouldn't last forever.

His words echoed in her mind. *Bad things don't last forever.*

She smiled and tapped reply on the message. She simply told him that all was forgiven and that she couldn't say no to coffee. *Or him.* But she didn't tell him that.

Chapter Twelve

WORKING ON CARS HAD BEEN CARTER'S WAY of avoiding the outside world. But now, he couldn't focus on the job long enough without thinking about Hannah.

Her words had done something to him. They had made him think about the life he'd had growing up and how fortunate he should feel because he had been provided for with a roof over his head and a love-filled place to call home.

The fact that Hannah hadn't been given the same kind of love upset him. She hadn't said a word about her upbringing, other than her relationship with her estranged sister, but she didn't have to say anything else for Carter to hear what she wasn't saying.

He'd left the shop last night after sending her a message. He hadn't been too sure about what to expect once he hit send, but he needed Hannah to know that he hadn't meant to pry into her business.

Of course, he'd left out the part that he couldn't stop thinking about her and wanting to make sure she was okay—both physically and emotionally. He hated seeing her cry, knowing there wasn't a thing he could do about it. Well, at least not yet, anyway.

Hopping into his truck, he headed toward the bed and breakfast. He felt fairly confident that today would go better than any other had recently. The snowstorm that had been moving into town out of the northwest had shifted its path and was headed directly south according to the weatherman's latest report on the radio.

He pulled the truck into the driveway leading to the bed and breakfast and parked as close to the house as he could. He debated on whether or not to leave it running, but killed the engine two seconds later and hopped out.

The snow-covered gravel crunched under his feet as he made his way to the porch. He could hear the dog barking around back, more than likely chasing the geese, Gus and Gertie, while Catie was preoccupied with entertaining Hannah and Grace.

It cracked him up to know that Ethan and Duke had won his sister's heart after a rough few weeks staying at the bed and breakfast. But, like all the others had said, Fran called it and she'd been right about them. Carter couldn't think of anyone better for his sister. Actually, that could be said for all of his sisters. He and his brothers no longer had to worry.

He rapped his knuckles against the wooden door and didn't have to wait too long before Catie answered and peeked her head out. "Carter," she said, pulling the door open and motioning for him to step inside. "How many times do I have to tell you that you don't have to knock?"

She was scolding him for being polite, but then again, she had told him a million times, if not more, that he was always welcome to enter without knocking. When was he going to learn? Probably never.

"I'll continue to knock until the day I die, Cat," he said with a smug grin. He knew it got her riled up when he refused to listen. He was stubborn like that. It was a trait he inherited from his father. Each of the Mitchell siblings had their fair share of stubborness, but Carter was pretty sure that his trumped theirs.

"What are you doin' here, anyway?" Catie asked, trying to play it off like she didn't know why he was standing in the entryway of her house.

"I'm always welcome, remember?"

He shot her another smug grin and leaned against the wall. He glanced around, but didn't see any sign of Hannah or the baby.

"She's not here," Catie said as she caught him looking around.

"What?" he asked. "Why not? Where'd she go?"

Catie raised a brow and shot him a smirk of her own. "Gotcha."

He shook his head and crossed his arms over his chest. "Cut it out. Is she upstairs?"

"Yes," Catie said while laughing, "she told me that you'd be comin' to pick her up. I offered to watch Grace so the two of you can spend some more time getting to know each other."

He wanted to deny that those were his intentions, but Catie knew him better than the rest of the Mitchell siblings. She would call him out on his bluff faster than he could spit the words out.

"What do you have planned for this *date* of yours?" Catie teased, wiggling her eyebrows and laughing when he grabbed the decorative pillow from a nearby chair and tossed it at her. "What's the matter? The cat got your tongue, CarCar?"

He shook his head and tried to hide the heat he felt creeping into his cheeks. He couldn't remember the last time he'd gone on a date. Sure, he'd had his nights out with the guys that ended with a few women here and there wanting to go home with him, but he wasn't that type of guy. He wanted something serious or nothing at all. There wasn't any sense in wasting time on something if it wasn't going to last.

He'd been there. Done that. There was nothing easy about falling in love with a woman just to watch her walk away without the slightest care in the world, all while pretending it didn't bother him.

He shook his head to clear his thoughts.

"Hey," Hannah called out as she made her way down the stairs with Grace in her arms.

"Mornin'."

He watched as Hannah handed Grace off to his sister and smiled when she looked over at him. "Let me grab something and I'll be ready to go."

He quickly nodded and waited patiently for her to return. When she came back to the front entrance, she was carrying her purse and wearing shoes. He pointed at the purse and said, "You won't be needin' that."

Hannah glanced at Catie and back at him, but he stood his ground. "I'm payin' this time."

She tried to argue with him, telling him it wasn't necessary. That she could afford her own coffee and he really didn't have to pay for it. But he insisted without budging until she finally agreed to leave her purse at the house.

He reached for the door and pulled it open as she gave Grace one last kiss on the cheek. "I'll see you after a bit. I'll be right back, okay?" she whispered. "Thank you, Catie," she called over her shoulder as she followed him out the door.

"Watch your step," he said, offering her the crook of his arm and smiling when she gladly accepted it. "It's a bit slick out here."

He didn't let her go until they were at the passenger side of his truck and he was able to help her climb in without falling. The winter months were terrible in Maple Glen, and he knew the fun was just beginning now that they were creeping into December.

Silence filled the truck, making him wonder if maybe there was a chance that she hadn't forgiven him for stepping over the line and pushing things a little too far in their conversation.

"Has the part for my car arrived yet?"

Her question was short and to the point. It didn't leave any room for guessing what she was getting at either. She was wanting to get the heck out of Dodge, and there was nothing he could do to stop her.

The sting of the reality of the situation slapped him in the face as he turned the key in the ignition and shifted into drive. After getting to know her and realizing there was something about her that he couldn't walk away from, he didn't like the fact that she was still planning to leave town... but he knew from the start that was her plan.

For some reason, Carter struggled to remember she had once been a stranded stranger on the side of the road. On her way to a place far from Maple Glen.

"Is that a no?" she asked, quirking her brow and waiting for him to give an answer.

"Not yet, but once we get to the coffee shop, I'll take a look at the tracking link and see where it's at."

"Okay."

"Okay," he echoed, guiding the truck onto Main Street and parking in front of his aunt's shop. The open sign flashed in the window, and it looked like his sister, Cara, and Autumn were already there and settled in their booth for girl talk.

"Do you like to gossip over coffee?"

Hannah snapped her head in his direction and gave him a puzzled look. He chuckled as he pointed to the booth right inside the large open window. "That's what they're doin'," he said. "I'm not sure how it all got started, but somewhere along the way, my sisters decided it would be a good idea to sit at the coffee shop all hours of the morning and talk."

Hannah's eyes focused straight ahead as she watched the booth full of women.

"I'd never heard so much talkin' in my life until I started coming here for coffee," he admitted with a light chuckle. "I would've thought they'd run out of things to talk about by now, but nope."

Hannah's lips pulled into a soft smile, and he wondered if maybe there would be a day that he would find her sitting among the others, laughing and talking over her coffee.

"Shall we?" he asked, pulling the handle and stepping out of the driver's seat. He made his way to her side and offered the crook of his arm once again. He would never tire of being a gentleman, no matter how many women broke his heart. "Maybe I'll introduce you to them and you can sit with them the next time you're in here?"

She didn't seem to mind his suggestion, but at the same time, he caught a glimpse of hesitation.

Something that told him that she wouldn't make it a habit.

He pushed the door open and followed Hannah inside. The sleigh bells rang out, announcing their arrival to the crowd that filled the small coffee shop. He glanced around and was impressed with the number of people who were still coming into his aunt's place for coffee in the mornings.

"It's a bit packed," Hannah said, pressing against him and trying to make room for the passerby.

"What do you say we just grab our coffee to go, then?" he asked, wrapping his arm around her and guiding her toward the counter when she agreed to go along with his plan. He knew that his aunt would more than likely understand why they weren't sticking around.

"Hey, Aunt Fran," he called out as they approached the counter. Fran was hustling around behind the counter, making her way from one end to the other while still managing to take orders and prepare them, too.

"You're gonna have to speak up if you're tryin' to talk to me, Carter. I can't hear ya over all this noise," she called out over the coffee pots as she wiped the sweat from her brow. "It's good to see the two of you. What do the two of you have planned for the day?"

Carter glanced over at Hannah who offered a subtle shrug. He smiled and turned back to Fran. "Not sure yet, but we figured we'd stop and get some coffee.

But from the looks of it, we might have to take it to go."

Fran made her way to their end of the counter and leaned against it, trying her best to hear what he was saying. "What can I get ya?"

Hannah took a small step toward the counter and told Fran what she wanted while Carter knew that his aunt already knew what he wanted.

"Comin' right up," Fran called out, making her way to the other end of the counter once again.

"Why doesn't she have anyone helping her out?"

"We've been asking her that for years now," Carter explained, gently placing his hand at the small of her back as he guided her to a vacant space near the kitchen doorway. "Cara had been helping out quite a bit when she first moved back from Minnesota, but then her photography and wedding planning business with Autumn picked up steam and there went that."

Hannah glanced over at Cara and Autumn before she said, "You weren't joking when you said everyone in your family is a business owner."

Carter's lips pulled into a proud smile. His family had made a name for themselves around Maple Glen. It was something to be proud of. "Not one bit."

"Is there anything your family can't do?"

"Afraid not." He joked before correcting himself, "Absolutely. My brother, Clayton, can't figure out math to save his life, but he can carve a hog within minutes."

Hannah's eyes widened, and he figured he'd better explain. "He owns the meat locker and deli across the street. My parents handed it down to him when they decided to retire."

Hannah slowly nodded and said, "Okay, then. That makes me feel better. I was starting to think that your family is one of those who live in the Hallmark kind of movies."

Carter chuckled and said, "Close, but not quite."

Fran called out behind them as she held up their coffees. "You two have a good day. And try not to do anything I wouldn't do," she said with a wink as she handed them their drinks. She paused for a minute and asked, "Where's the little one?"

Carter looked at Hannah then back to his aunt. "Catie offered to watch her for a little while."

Fran's eyes lit up, and she nodded with a knowing smile. "Good," she said. "Maybe that little one of yours will cause her to catch some baby fever."

Carter shook his head at his aunt's antics. He wasn't quite sure his sister and Ethan were ready for one of their own just yet. Everyone in his family made it a point to at least be engaged before thinking about having babies, but then again, it wasn't his business and he liked it that way.

Besides, he had other things to think about—like taking Hannah out and having some fun of their own. Snowmobiles and all.

Chapter Thirteen

HANNAH TAGGED ALONG WITH CARTER AND climbed into the front seat. She watched him as he made his way around the front of the truck and hopped in next to her, fumbling the key into the ignition.

"Where to now?" she asked, taking a long pull from her caramel-flavored coffee. She had changed her mind on sticking to just one thing—even though she loved frappuccinos, she wanted something not so cold.

Carter offered a subtle shrug and shifted the truck in reverse before backing out of the parking spot. "You'll see."

"Back to the B and B?"

Carter's lips parted as though he was about to say something but had changed his mind as he focused on the snow-covered roads ahead of them.

"I'm actually loving it here," she said with a smile.

For the first time in nearly six months, Hannah felt relaxed and hopeful—something she had almost given up on. "I'm going to be sad when it's time to leave."

From the corner of her eye, she witnessed Carter's jaw clench. She knew it would be hard for both of them when the time came to say goodbye, despite the short amount of time they'd spent together. The last thing she wanted, when everything was said and done, was heartbreak and hard feelings toward one another.

She could tell that Carter cared about her and Grace. His actions said it all. She'd never met a man willing to do anything and everything for someone like her.

"Who said anything about leavin'?" he asked, tossing her a quick wink. "Who says that you have to leave?"

"Me," she said, knowing it wasn't what Carter wanted to hear. "I don't really have a choice. I can't..."

Hannah allowed her words to trail off and her thoughts to run wild. She didn't want to allow reality to ruin the day. She wanted to sit back and enjoy a day of carefree entertainment or whatever Carter had in mind, without overthinking and without emotions running high. She needed down-time—an escape.

If only for a minute.

"I think you'll like what I have in mind," Carter said, focusing his attention back on the road as he guided the truck along the winding roads heading out of Maple Glen. "There's no other day more perfect than today."

Hannah smiled as she relaxed into the seat. "Even with the cold winds blowing and the snow falling?"

Carter nodded. "Even then."

"How much longer?" she asked impatiently. She'd be the first to admit that patience wasn't one of her strengths. Curiosity and impatience always got the best of her and left her asking a thousand questions. "Are you sure that you're not taking me somewhere just to kill me? Should I be worried?"

Carter grunted as his hands gripped the steering wheel. "It's a little late to be wondering about all that, don't ya think?"

He was right, but thankfully, she'd meant it as a joke and was able to laugh about it. "True."

"Besides," he said with a smirk, "even if I were a bad guy, I don't think I'd be able to kill you."

Hannah's cheeks heated, and her heart skipped a beat. "That's the sweetest thing anyone's ever said to me, Carter Mitchell."

He chuckled and shook his head. "And here I thought I wasn't a romantic kind of guy."

"Well, I don't know about all that," she said with a grin of her own. She couldn't help but tease him. He was fun to pick on, and it was helping her break away from the stress she was under.

With a subtle shrug, Carter said, "Fair enough."

"So... are you going to tell me where we're headed?"

"You'll see in just a minute."

She turned her attention back to the road in front of them while looking at their surroundings, searching for a clue as to where they were going and what Carter had in mind. Surprised that she found herself more excited than nervous, Hannah smiled on the inside.

"Three... Two..." Carter's counting caught her attention, pulling her away from searching for the answer. "One."

Carter pointed ahead of them as he pulled off the highway and into the driveway belonging to a large cabin positioned several feet away from the main road. Hannah tossed him a puzzled look as she took in the view.

"A cabin?"

Carter smiled with another subtle shrug. "Not just any cabin, but my brother's cabin."

Hannah nodded. It only made sense that his family would own a cabin, too. The Mitchell family was well-established as far as she could tell, but they weren't like any of the business owners she'd known in Chicago.

The Mitchell family was different. They might have been running successful businesses, but as far as Hannah could tell, they didn't let their money talk. They stayed humble, but proud, while taking opportunities to help their community as needed.

"Okay," Hannah said, quirking a brow. "But why here?"

Carter shot her an untelling look that said it all—she would have to wait and see.

"Come on," he said, motioning for her to hop out of the truck and follow him along a snow-covered walkway. Hannah's feet slipped out from underneath her, but thanks to Carter and his quick reflexes, he caught her before she landed in the snow.

"Thanks," she whispered, righting herself before continuing her walk with Carter.

"My pleasure," Carter said, resting his hand on her lower back as they walked toward a large shed positioned on the other side of the cabin.

"Is your brother here?" Hannah asked, looking around for any sign of life and realizing that she and Carter were all alone in the middle of the woods. The thought was both nerve-wracking and exhilarating. "Will he be mad that we're here?"

Carter shook his head and motioned for Hannah to follow him to the shed. He slid a key into the lock and smiled. "Don't worry. Clayton's already given me the okay."

Carter opened the shed door and stepped inside, taking hold of Hannah's hand and guiding her inside. "Besides," he said, "this place belonged to my parents before they retired and moved to Florida. Clayton just got lucky because he's the oldest."

Hannah laughed at Carter's remark. "Do I hear

some jealousy in your tone, Carter?" she teased, taking one more step into the shed and looking around.

Toolboxes, lawn mowers, more tools, and something covered with a tarp crowded the spacious shed. "Wow," was the only word she could manage as she took in the sight of everything.

Carter walked to the tarp and gave it a quick pull, revealing a—

"Snowmobile?"

"Yep," he responded with a grin.

"A snowmobile?" she asked again.

"Yes, a snowmobile," Carter said, quirking a brow at her, and she knew what he was thinking before he asked it. "You know what a snowmobile is, right? You take it out in the snow and ride around on it…"

Hannah laughed out loud as she walked over to it. "Yes, I know what it is," she admitted, slapping his arm. "I've just never been on one."

"Never?"

Hannah shook her head. "Never. I'm a city girl, remember?"

Carter nodded and uncovered the snowmobile the rest of the way. "What do you say we change that?"

"You and me?" Hannah asked with a nervous laugh. "On that?"

Carter shrugged. "Why not? I think it's a good idea. It'll be fun."

Hannah thought about it for a minute. Out of all of the things she had in mind when they had left the coffee shop, riding on a snowmobile wasn't one of them. The thought of riding horses had crossed her mind, but of course, she wouldn't know how to get on one of those, let alone ride one.

"Do you wanna find somethin' else to do?" Carter asked, taking a step toward her. "I'm sure we can find somethin' else to do around here, but I still think playin' in the snow beats everything else."

"Playing in the snow, huh?" Hannah glanced over at the snowmobile and back at Carter. "That does sound fun."

"So it's a yes?" he asked with a wide smile.

She nodded, unsure of what she was getting herself into, but allowed Carter to lead the way.

He hadn't steered her the wrong way yet, so she had no choice but to go along with him. She just hoped that she could trust him not to hurt her—heart and all.

"HANG ON TIGHT," CARTER HOLLERED OVER his shoulder. He had pulled out of the shed and tossed her a helmet, along with a snowsuit. She wasn't so sure that she wanted to put a helmet on, or even the suit, but Carter told her it was all about safety first. "Are you ready?"

"I'm ready," Hannah said, wrapping her arms around Carter and leaning into his back. She closed her eyes and prayed to God that she wouldn't get hurt. She'd never been brave enough to try new things. She was always living in her comfort zone.

Until now.

Now she had no choice but to move forward and brave a new life while trying to make ends meet. It was no different than hopping on a snowmobile with Carter and allowing herself to have fun.

"Okay, hang on," Carter hollered over the loud roar of the snowmobile's engine. Hannah nodded and clung tightly to him, preparing herself for takeoff and not knowing what to expect.

The engine relaxed to a low-humming idle before Carter shifted and gave it gas. Hannah closed her eyes, caught off guard by the motion, but slowly opened them as Carter guided the snowmobile toward an open field.

Though she was unsure of the adventure awaiting her, once they got going, she wondered why it had taken her so long. She could only imagine what other things she could enjoy before leaving Maple Glen.

Maple Glen was the complete opposite of the city she grew up in. Hannah was still trying to adapt to the small, quiet town with an occasional honking of a horn here and there or a group of kids passing by the bed and breakfast in their snow gear, pulling sleds behind them and calling out who could get to their destination the fastest.

Of course, Hannah still loved Chicago. It was her

hometown. The only town she'd known for the last twenty-three years. The crime rate was off the charts depending on the time of day, but at the same time, there were things that weren't so bad—like with every city or town.

She thought about Ashley. After everything that had happened, including the argument they'd had before Ashley left the apartment, it wasn't like her sister to not check in. They'd had several arguments over the last ten years, but not one argument had ended up like this last one.

Hannah tucked her chin down, allowing the zipped jacket to guard against the cold wind nipping at her bare skin.

The engine quieted and Carter hollered over his shoulder, "What do you say we check out the river?"

Hannah's heart raced at the thought of going by the river. She didn't like water. Not since she almost drowned trying to save Ashley from drowning in their neighbor's pool. To this day, she still didn't know what happened or how it happened. She could only thank God and the angels who'd helped them.

"Just as long as you promise not to get too close to the water's edge," she said, praying Carter would listen. Panic closed in and crept into her voice, causing it to shake as she said, "I don't like water."

The engine died down as the snowmobile slowed to a stop. Carter took his helmet off and turned to face her. Hannah followed suit and removed hers as well.

She wasn't sure what was going through his mind as his brown eyes focused on hers. Maybe he thought she was a scaredy cat. She wouldn't argue with that.

"Hannah," he said, causing her heart to beat hard against her ribs. Her breath caught, realizing they were close enough for her to feel the warmth of his breath on her face. She relaxed her arms, releasing the death grip her arms had formed around him. "I won't let anything happen to you. Trust me. Besides, the river is frozen solid."

She felt vulnerable. Panic set in, and it got the best of her—like always.

"Hey," he said, reaching out and placing an open hand on her cheek, "I promise."

Catie's words flashed through Hannah's mind. Carter didn't make promises he didn't intend to keep.

Hannah reached up and rested her hand on top of his, not wanting the moment to end. She wasn't sure when the line blurred between being strangers and something more, but she didn't care.

She looked into his eyes, studying them for as long as time allowed. He leaned in, closing the distance between them. His breath warm against her lips. Closing her eyes, she leaned into him and met his lips with hers.

The kiss was everything she thought it would be as she allowed herself to let go of every worry she had and enjoy the moment. Just her and Carter.

No thoughts of being homeless. No thoughts

about being broke and having nothing but the clothes she'd brought and a few things for her niece.

Lost in the kiss, Hannah let go of everything holding her back and allowed herself to be free—if only for a minute, she could feel something other than pain and weakness.

Carter pulled back, brushing his hand through her hair and tucking a loose strand behind her ear. She smiled, speechless. There was so much she wanted to say but didn't have the words to say them. So instead of ruining the moment with rambling, Hannah inhaled a deep breath and released it slowly.

"Ready for more?" Carter asked with a playful grin. Hannah wouldn't say no to another kiss like that, but she soon realized he wasn't talking about kissing. He was preparing to take her on the ride of her lifetime.

It was now or never.

"I'm ready."

Chapter Fourteen

THEY SPENT A FEW HOURS ON THE RIVER before Carter decided to head back to the cabin. He knew that it was nearing supper time based on the sun setting behind them. If he had it his way, he would have stayed out all night with Hannah.

But it wasn't up to him. She had a baby waiting for her back at the house, and he needed to get the snowmobile put away before dark since the broken headlight hadn't been fixed yet—for which he took the blame.

Clayton had called him about it a couple of weeks back, asking him to fix it in his spare time. In Carter's defense, he hadn't found the time. Especially with Vince's vehicle in the shop for the last three weeks needing an overhaul on the motor.

Carter steered the snowmobile along the path they'd originally set out on. Hannah's arms were wrapped tightly around his waist, and he was more than thankful that she trusted him enough to take her out on the ice.

"The scenery is so beautiful around here," she said over the whir of the motor before Carter parked in the driveway right out front of the shed.

Carter yanked off his helmet and turned to find Hannah doing the same. The snow hadn't stopped since they'd set out on their adventure, and the temperature was steadily dropping if the frost on his truck's windshield was any indication.

"That it is," Carter admitted. "That's one of the reasons I love it out here so much."

Hannah climbed off the snowmobile and smiled at him. "I wouldn't have thought of you as being a nature-loving kind of guy."

Carter grunted with a shake of his head before firing up the snowmobile and pulling it into the shed. He wondered what would have prompted Hannah into thinking about him in the first place, let alone branding him as a certain kind of guy.

He climbed off the machine and headed out of the shed, walking toward Hannah. "What kind of guy did you think I was?"

She offered a subtle shrug, and a soft smile spread across her lips. He knew that look by now and what it meant. "I'd rather not say."

Carter had a feeling that it wasn't too good if she was trying to avoid answering him, but curiosity got the best of him as always. "Come on," he pleaded, "I've got thick skin. I can handle it."

She took a step toward him, and he watched as a shiver ran through her. He quickly locked up the shed and headed for his truck. There was no sense in making her stand out in the cold any longer than necessary.

"Let's hop in," he said, motioning toward the truck. He rested a hand on her lower back as he walked alongside her. "Once we're warmed up, you can tell me what kind of guy you think I am."

Hannah shook her head but climbed into his truck without saying a word. He knew the night they'd met that he might have given the impression that he wasn't much for talking and making pleasantries, but he blamed that on the wall he'd built to protect himself from the outside world.

"I'll admit that at first you didn't come across as being a city girl," he said, climbing into the driver's seat and buckling in. He offered a cheesy grin, knowing that his words might have awakened a buried frustration inside of her by the look on her face. With a furrowed brow, she turned to him and asked, "What's that supposed to mean?"

He swallowed against the lump that was forming in his throat. The last thing he wanted to do was make waves when things were going smoothly between them. He held up his hands and said, "Nothin' bad, I swear."

She crossed her arms over her chest and leaned against the door. "Good, then you should be able to tell me."

A quirk of her brow told him that she wasn't as upset as she was curious, and she wasn't going to let it go until he told her.

Lights flashed through the back window, pulling their attention behind them. "Saved by the Chief Deputy," he mumbled, offering Hannah a sly grin. "It's all fun and games until the cops show up."

He opened the door and climbed out. Once his feet hit the snow covered gravel, he missed the warmth of the truck. Missed the closeness he'd felt with Hannah sitting next to him on the bench seat.

"What can I do for ya, Vince?" he asked, offering a coy smile and knowing the guy hadn't always been too fond of Carter. The feeling had been mutual.

Vince glanced at the passenger side of Carter's truck as he approached the tailgate. "Just heard some noise along the river and figured I'd come investigate."

Carter looked over his shoulder at Hannah and turned back to Vince. "Nothin' going on here except taking the snowmobile for a ride along the river."

Vince nodded, slowly examining the scene in front of him. Carter had seen that look before. It hadn't been all that long ago that Vince had welcomed himself into the Mitchell family and had come head to head with Carter. Carter admitted he had been a little too cocky when it came to talking with Vince. In all honesty, he was lucky that Vince hadn't acted against Carter's threats. He hadn't been in the right to threaten anyone, especially someone who wore a badge and carried a gun for a living.

"How's Cara and the little one?" he asked, trying to make conversation.

Thankfully, all of that was behind them since Carter realized how happy Vince made Cara. And Vince's promise to take care of her didn't hurt. Carter didn't believe in all of the mushy love stuff. He'd been there and done that once during high school, but it had been short lived once college admissions took place and his high school sweetheart believed Carter could no longer give her what she needed. It hadn't mattered that he'd purchased a ring and gotten down on one knee. He still walked away with a broken heart and a load of debt for a ring he couldn't give away.

"They're good," Vince said, feet standing shoulder width apart and his thumbs hooked in his gun belt. "Who's in the front seat?"

Carter glanced over his shoulder and motioned for Hannah to hop out. He waited until she was standing beside him and said, "Hannah, this is Chief Deputy Vince Bradley. Vince, this is Hannah."

He watched as Hannah held out her hand in a nervous fashion and shook Vince's hand. He wasn't sure why she seemed so nervous, but brushed it off as a normal reaction.

Silence hung around the three of them as Vince

studied Hannah. Carter had no way of knowing what Vince was thinking, but he'd ask him about it later for sure. "It's nice to meet you, Vince," Hannah said, taking a step back and rubbing her hands together to keep them warm.

"Same to you," Vince said, keeping his voice low and his face indecipherable. He turned his attention to Carter and asked, "When do you think I'll have my SUV back?"

Carter wasn't sure how long it would take him, but with Ethan's help, he didn't think it would take too much longer. "I've been stuck driving Ol' Jalopy," Vince said, hooking a thumb over his shoulder toward the ancient squad car that had to be older than Carter. "I'm getting kind of tired of driving around town in it, ya know?"

Carter offered a light chuckle and said, "I've been pretty busy lately at the shop, but with Ethan's help, I don't think it'll be too much longer. End of the week, maybe? Give or take a day or so?"

Carter wasn't blind. He noticed the look Vince gave him and Hannah when he'd mentioned being busy. "Sounds good," Vince said. He looked at Hannah and asked, "What brings you to Maple Glen?"

"I..." Hannah started, but looked to Carter before she continued, "I was on my way to see my friend when my car broke down."

Recognition lit up in Vince's face as he pointed at

Hannah. "So you're the one who Fran's been talking about lately?"

Again, Hannah looked at Carter. With a laugh, he said, "More than likely."

Vince gave a knowing nod and said, "You're the one with the baby, then?"

Hannah fidgeted nervously beside Carter, and he knew that the questioning was making her uncomfortable, but what he wasn't sure about was why. Vince no longer stared at her with concern, and he wasn't interrogating her with his questions. He was back to being his normal self and seemed to have put his job aside for now.

"Yep, that's me," she answered.

Carter saw her shiver from the corner of his eye and used that as a way to end the awkward tension between them. "Well, I suppose," he said, taking a step back and offering a subtle wave to Vince, "I ought to get her where it's warm. I'll let ya know when we get your vehicle done. Like I said, it shouldn't take too long now that I've got Ethan to help me out."

Vince nodded. "Sounds good. I'll see you guys later. Have a good night."

Carter watched Vince walk back to his car and climb into the driver's seat. He had a feeling that there was something Vince wanted to say, but it didn't matter now. If the guy was upset about the time it was taking Carter to fix his engine, then he could take it elsewhere.

But then again, Carter couldn't afford to let the job go somewhere else. He needed all the money he could get. The winter months were a rough patch for Carter, and the last thing he needed was to lose business.

"How long has he been waiting?" Hannah asked, watching Vince drive off down the gravel road.

"About three weeks," Carter answered honestly. He had no reason to lie about it. He had been on his own until recently when he decided he needed to hire a part-timer to come in three days a week. But even that hadn't been a good decision since he was hurting for money and couldn't really afford to pay anyone more than a few hundred dollars.

"Any news on the part for my car?"

"Let's hop in the truck, and I'll check the tracking on it," he said, motioning toward his truck that had been running the whole time they'd been standing outside.

He pulled his phone out of the pocket of his flannel jacket and tapped on the link that had been sent just two days prior. The results weren't looking too bright. "Looks like it won't be here for a while."

Hannah looked over at him with a raised brow. "A while? How long is *a while*?"

"It looks like it might be stuck in the snowstorm," he said, taking his best guess.

"That's just great."

He wanted to ask her why she was so upset. He

knew that she had been planning to visit a friend, but he couldn't understand why that was so upsetting when she seemed to be enjoying herself there in Maple Glen. And before they knew it, the next winter storm would be coming through, and then what? Would Hannah take the chance of traveling in a winter storm and risk an accident?

Instead of saying anything, he apologized. Everything was out of his control whether he liked it or not.

"What do you say we get out of here?"

With a quick nod of her head, he shifted into drive and guided the truck onto the highway. He would drop her off at the bed and breakfast before heading over to his shop. He might be able to get an hour or two of work done on Vince's SUV before calling it a night.

Chapter Fifteen

HANNAH WASN'T SURE HOW TO FEEL ABOUT the part for her car being stuck inside a box somewhere en route to Maple Glen. She wanted her car fixed and she wanted to get to Tara's, but at the same time, she couldn't deny the feelings she'd felt when she was wrapped in Carter's arms.

Not to mention the kiss they'd shared.

Shaking her head, she pulled her phone out of her pocket as she rocked Grace in the chair. Catie had no complaints about Grace while Hannah had been gone. Hannah had been relieved to hear that. It had done her good to get out of the house, considering the coffee had been good and the time she'd spent with Carter had been well worth it.

Catie stood from sitting beside Hannah and Grace. "I think I'm going to start somethin' to eat. Are you hungry?"

Hannah nodded eagerly, especially after listening to her stomach growl for the last hour or so since Carter had dropped her off. He hadn't said much when they arrived at the bed and breakfast, but he also hadn't allowed her to leave without another quick kiss.

She sent a message to Tara. She wanted to let her know that her car would be taking longer than expected to get fixed. She included the latest update in regards to the part that was needed.

Propping Grace's bottle against her chest, Hannah was able to continue her texting conversation with Tara, who had replied back within seconds of Hannah sending the first message.

Do you need me to come and get you? I can have Brad keep an eye on the kids.

Hannah thought about her best friend's offer. It only made sense that Tara would make an offer like that without hesitation. They had been the best of friends since grade school, and other than a few fights that involved bickering rather than actual fighting, Hannah couldn't think of a time they weren't friends.

It's getting late and I don't feel right making you drive all the way here.

Before waiting for her response, Hannah quickly typed another message.

Besides, they're talking about a snowstorm moving in. I don't want to worry about you getting caught in it while trying to help me.

A ping sounded, followed by a low vibration as another message from Tara popped up.

Don't be silly. I've driven in worse conditions than a blizzard. There's nothing I wouldn't do when it comes to helping you. YOU know that.

Hannah teared up while reading the last message. Tara had a point. Hannah remembered a time they'd both skipped class in their junior year of high school and decided to sneak out of town to hang out with a couple of boys that Tara had met online. Looking back, it had been fun and they had both felt invincible while on the road. Or at least until a tornado came from out of nowhere and almost wiped them out.

Hannah cringed at the thought. Even though they'd just gotten their licenses and barely had any experience behind the wheel aside from attending driver's education, Tara handled the beat-up Cavalier like a pro.

Ever since that day, Hannah knew better than to question Tara's driving skills. Whether it was Tara's ability to maintain control of the car, or a stroke of luck, they were both thankful to be alive to tell the story to their own kids one day.

Kids. The thought crossed Hannah's mind. She hadn't thought about having kids of her own. Not since she'd played the MASH game on the school bus as a teenager, anyway. Tara had always been the one who swore she'd have her own football team before she turned thirty, but Hannah had refused to believe it.

Another ping followed by a vibration, pulling Hannah out of her thoughts.

Okay, so what's the plan?

Hannah didn't have a plan. She'd been wanting to get out of Maple Glen as soon as she was able to, but now everything seemed to be working against her. She couldn't just leave her car in Carter's shop. Not only that... she couldn't leave, period.

Her mind thought about the moments she'd shared with Carter. Kissing him had been a breath of fresh air. A promise that everything would be okay.

I think I'll wait it out. There's no telling how long it'll take for the part to get here, but Carter promises to fix my car as soon as it arrives.

She hit send, feeling confident in her decision to stay.

Carter huh? First name basis?

The mechanic. She quickly responded, not feeling up to explaining. She would at some point, but not tonight.

Okay... are you sure that you don't want me to come and get you?

Hannah chuckled as she replied to the message.

Yes, I'm sure. I'll call you tomorrow, okay?

She set her phone down on the end table and looked down at Grace. At some point in time while Hannah had been busy messaging her friend, Grace had dozed off and had spit the bottle out of her mouth. Formula had continued to drip along Grace's neckline, soaking both her outfit and the chair's fabric under Hannah's arm. "Shoot," Hannah said, switching Grace to her other arm as she reached for the burp rag. She should have paid closer attention. After all this time, a person would have thought she'd have a handle on taking care and watching over Grace. Hannah was failing.

"Need some help?" Catie asked, walking into the living room and offering to hold Grace. Hannah gladly accepted her offer as she handed Grace over.

"I can't believe that happened," Hannah grumbled and mumbled under her breath. Catie watched in fascination while rocking Grace back and forth in her arms. Catie was a pro at taking care of Grace—of kids in general. Hannah had noticed that about Catie right away.

"Don't worry about it," Catie said, waving a hand toward the chair. "It's not the first time, and it definitely won't be the last. It'll dry."

Hannah relaxed a bit as she dabbed the chair with the rag. Catie was so laid back and easy going. The complete opposite of Hannah. "I'm sorry," Hannah said, still trying her best to rid the formula from the fabric. "Do you have anything I can clean it with?"

Instead of directing Hannah to a cupboard containing cleaning products, Catie ignored her and changed the subject. "How was your date with Carter?"

"Oh... it wasn't a... I—"

Catie interrupted her with a laugh. "You can't tell me there's nothin' going on with you two," Catie said, pointing a finger at Hannah. "I know for a fact that my brother likes you, and tell me if I'm wrong, but you like him too."

Hannah stood with a soaked rag in one hand and a look of shock on her face.

"All I have to do is call up my Aunt Fran, and she'll tell me all about it, I'm sure," Catie threatened with a smile on her face. Hannah tossed the rag into a nearby laundry basket. "You might as well tell me what I already know. There's no sense in denyin' it."

Hannah wasn't trying to deny anything. She was just trying to find the words to tell Catie all about the time she'd spent with Carter and how much fun it had been. How Carter was able to take her fear of the water away while they rode along the frozen river. The fear of falling through the ice had crossed her mind, but only for a second because Carter promised that he knew what he was doing. He wouldn't take her out on the ice if he didn't think it was safe enough to do so.

"Trust me," Catie said, pulling Hannah from her thoughts, "my brother has been hiding out in that shop of his for a while now, and we weren't sure what it would take to get him to venture out."

Hannah thought about Carter. Sure, he seemed to be the workaholic type, but as far as being a hermit? Hannah wouldn't believe it.

"But I think we just found out," Catie said, setting

Grace down in the playpen and covering her with a blanket.

Hannah watched in awe as Catie tucked Grace in and walked back over to the couch. She waited for Catie to sit down before taking a seat herself. "What's that?"

Catie's face lit up as she smiled at Hannah. "You."

"Me?"

"Yes," Catie insisted. "You were able to draw him out of his cave, and that speaks volumes. He likes you, Hannah."

Hannah felt the heat creep into her cheeks. She wouldn't deny liking him as well, but what was she supposed to say? She was leaving as soon as her car was fixed. She had been pretending Grace was her own daughter instead of her niece. In a way, Hannah felt like she was living a double life and not telling the whole truth.

Carter didn't know the real Hannah. And she wasn't sure if she wanted him to.

Chapter Sixteen

AFTER DROPPING HANNAH OFF AT CATIE'S, Carter decided it would be best to lay low for a while and get Vince's SUV done. Vince hadn't seemed too happy about having to wait another few days.

But then again, he hadn't seemed too happy about Hannah either. Carter's mind flashed back to the conversation they'd had outside the cabin and the look on Vince's face when Hannah seemed nervous.

If Carter didn't know any better, he would have thought Hannah was hiding something. But she couldn't have been hiding anything because Carter would have known by now, wouldn't he?

He shrugged it off, turning his attention back to the engine block he was currently working on. He'd come a long way in three weeks with this pain in the neck engine, but not as far as he would have liked to get. The county depended on him to get the vehicle repaired, and that's exactly what he would do.

It wasn't like he had wanted it to take as long as it had in the first place. He liked to get cars in and out as quickly as possible. A quick turnaround promised a good reputation and happy customers. Happy customers meant positive word of mouth and free marketing.

Every business owner depended on happy customers. It was a guarantee to help keep a business open and running.

Carter was confident that Vince wouldn't run his mouth about how long it had taken Carter to fix the deputy's vehicle, but it didn't settle the unease Carter felt with the whole situation.

The bell above the door rang and footsteps made their way over to Carter, who was elbows deep in engine grease and wrenches.

"Hey, need some help?"

Carter looked up and was relieved to see Ethan standing next to him. "I could use a lot, actually."

He tried to joke about his predicament, but the look on Ethan's face told him that he knew better. There wouldn't be a shared laugh with Ethan when things were getting serious. "I heard Vince wants this back ASAP."

Carter grunted, scrubbing his hands on a rag he pulled out of his back pocket. "Who'd you hear that from?"

Ethan shrugged, not wanting to say, and sidled up next to the front end. "Tell me what to do," Ethan said, readying himself to do whatever Carter told him.

Carter brushed off Ethan's unwillingness to tell him who had mentioned Vince wanting his vehicle back and began guiding Ethan through the steps of repairing an engine. "You're a city guy through and through."

Carter's accusation came out in a huff, but he hadn't meant for it to sound as harsh as it did. Ethan tossed him a warning look and Carter shook his head. "Sorry, man, I didn't mean for it to sound like I'm slammin' ya."

Ethan nodded and busied himself with a few tools. "Actually, you're right. I am a city guy, but that doesn't mean I don't like getting my hands dirty every now and then."

Carter laughed and nodded. "You're right," he said, knowing it was best to let it go and move along to another conversation.

"How's business goin' over at the hardware store?" Carter asked, trying his best to stay focused on the task at hand and avoid upsetting his help. He needed Ethan's help now more than ever. He couldn't afford to have Ethan walk out and leave him hanging.

"It's going well, I guess," Ethan answered, cranking on the wrench and tightening a bolt.

Carter wondered what that was all about. The last he had heard was that Harold Davis was looking to retire soon and would be handing the business down to Ethan. "When's your gramps going to retire?"

Ethan grunted with a light chuckle. "Probably never. You and I both know that place is his pride and joy. He isn't going to give it up that easily."

Carter shrugged with a grin. "I guess, but what are you going to do if he doesn't retire?"

Ethan stepped back away from the front end and combed a hand through his hair. "I guess I haven't thought much about it. Catie's been keeping me fairly busy at the bed and breakfast. What with all the renovations and add-ons taking place within the next year or so. I don't think I have anything to worry about. Gramps can keep running the hardware store as long as he wants, I suppose. I'll just keep up with the demands of the B and B."

Carter chuckled again, handing Ethan the torque wrench. "Sounds like you've got it made, then."

Ethan smirked. "Yeah, I guess I do, huh? In more ways than just one."

The bell above the door rang and footsteps found their way toward Carter and Ethan. Vince approached the side of the SUV and offered a friendly, "Hey, how's it goin'?"

Carter poked his head out from under the hood and looked up at Vince. "Just finishin' up with it."

Carter pushed off the bumper and ran his hands through the dirty rag from his back pocket. "What's up?"

Vince's stance told Carter that the man didn't come to the shop for small talk. He was there on strict business. With a furrowed brow, Vince crossed his arms over his chest and asked, "How long has this Hannah been in town?"

Carter glanced back at Ethan, who was now stepping away from Vince's SUV and making his way over to the conversation. Carter shrugged. "I don't know. Not long," he said, tossing a look at Ethan and realizing he'd lost track of the days. "A couple of weeks, maybe?"

He looked at Ethan. "Has it even been that long?"

Ethan offered a quick shrug and turned toward Vince. "Why? What's goin' on?"

Ethan leaned against the hood of another vehicle while they waited for Vince to answer the question. Several thoughts ran through Carter's mind, but he still couldn't figure out why Vince was stuck on Hannah. What was it about Hannah that had Vince on alert?

"And how old is the baby she has with her?" Vince asked, moving along through his questions and ignoring Ethan's. Carter shot another glance at Ethan, questioning what was going on, but Ethan looked just as confused. Vince cleared his throat. He walked over to the isolated barstools and grabbed one for himself while Carter watched him.

"About six months or so," Carter spoke up, keeping his eyes on Vince and trying to figure out why he was asking questions about Hannah. "What's goin' on?"

Red flags shot up, alerting him to something he might have missed along the way of letting his guard down and trusting Hannah. She hadn't seemed to be the type who would be in trouble with the law. She seemed to take good care of Grace.

It didn't make sense that Vince would be dropping twenty questions from out of nowhere. Carter could only hope it wasn't as bad as it seemed.

"I know she's from Chicago," Vince stated, tapping a thumb against his chin as he studied something written in the notebook he had pulled out of his pocket a few minutes prior to sitting down. "Has she mentioned any family?"

Carter didn't want to beat around the bush any longer. If there was something going on that was causing concern, the man should just come right out and say it. Carter made an attempt to get it out of him, but since that didn't work, he tried plan B. "If you've got somethin' against her, why don't you just say it."

Vince looked up from his notes, studying Carter for a minute before glancing back down. "Trust me, it's nothing personal," Vince said, tapping his notebook and shaking his head. "It's just that there's a few things that aren't making sense to me about the whole situation."

Carter looked at Ethan, who offered nothing more than a shrug as he walked over and grabbed the last barstool and took a seat next to Vince. "What's not makin' sense?"

Ethan's question pulled Vince's attention away from his notes. "I guess it might not be much of anything—"

"Then why are you askin' all these questions?" Carter didn't mean for the words to come out in a huff, and he sure didn't want to get in an uproar over a few questions being asked about Hannah. But there was something that Vince wasn't telling him, and it was enough to send Carter's defenses into action. "Like I said," Carter spat, "if you've got somethin' against her—"

"Carter," Vince snapped, "I heard you. And I'm telling you that I don't have anything against her personally. I just find it odd that she's traveling alone with a baby and her family hasn't come to help her out."

Carter took a step back. He relaxed his hands at his sides and took a deep breath. If he was about to go rounds with Vince, the Chief Deputy, over Hannah, he needed to pull it together. Heat flushed his cheeks as he exhaled hot air.

"Listen," Vince said, standing from his seat and holding his hands up in defense. "I've got years of experience when it comes to this kind of stuff on the streets. If this wasn't some small town, we'd all be looking at Hannah a little bit differently."

Carter relaxed a bit as he leaned against a car's

front end. His thoughts raced back to the night he'd first met Hannah and the look on her face. She had been full of concern and dread about her car breaking down, but that hadn't thrown any red flags for Carter. Anyone with a baby in the backseat and stalled on the side of the road would be filled with panic.

"I'm just saying... if this was, let's say, Chicago," Vince said, keeping Carter's attention, "the police would be wondering what she's running from."

Carter ran a tense hand through his hair and shook his head. "She's not runnin' from anything. She would have told me."

Getting defensive wasn't helping anything, but Carter couldn't help it. He had spent time with her. He'd gotten to know her on a personal level. She wasn't a criminal. She had issues with her family, sure, but that didn't mean she was on the run. She hadn't committed a crime.

"Have you asked her about her family? Why they're not coming to help her out?" Vince asked, keeping his voice low and calm unlike Carter who felt his blood pressure spiking through the roof. "I'm just saying it's odd, is all."

Carter didn't know what Vince wanted him to say. He looked to Ethan and back to Vince, lost in his own thoughts and defense mode. He wouldn't have let his guard down with a criminal. "What do you think she did? What's she guilty of?"

Vince shrugged his broad shoulders and adjusted

his gun belt as he shifted his weight. "I'm not saying there was a crime committed. I'm just curious to know why a single mother is traveling alone in the middle of winter with a less-than-trustworthy car."

Carter shrugged. He was out of answers. He couldn't deny that he'd wondered the same thing when he was putting two and two together about Hannah. And, if he were to be honest, he still hadn't put all the pieces together. There were still a few things that didn't make sense.

"I can tell that you care about her, man," Vince said, lowering his voice and keeping the situation under control. Carter respected Vince, but he hated that he'd brought all these unanswered questions to the surface. "But if she's in trouble..."

"I'm not sure what kind of trouble she'd be in, but whatever," Carter mumbled, refusing to believe what was laid out in front of him.

"She could be running from an abusive—"

Carter held up his hand to stop Vince from saying another word. "She didn't have any bruises, and I think we all would have known by now if that were the case."

Vince shrugged. "Maybe, but that's not always how it works."

Carter's mind ran through the last few conversations he'd had with Hannah. She'd mentioned her relationship with her estranged sister, but other than that, nothing had stood out as suspicious to Carter.

Vince's radio squawked, and the dispatcher relayed something about a caller stating they saw a bear in their backyard. Vince gave a quick "ten-four" and clipped his radio back onto his belt. He turned to Carter and nodded at Ethan. "I didn't come here to start anything. That wasn't my intention," he said, furrowing his brow. "I just want to make sure everything's okay. I'm just doing the job I took an oath for, right?"

Carter nodded and accepted Vince's extended hand for a quick handshake. Carter would let Vince do his job, but that didn't mean he had to like it. He hated to think that Hannah was hiding something from him.

"Give me a call when I can come and get Bertha, alright?" Vince asked with a slight chuckle as he headed for the door. As he approached the door, he called out, "I'll see you guys later."

"Yeah, later," Carter mumbled behind him as he watched Vince walk out the door. He turned toward Ethan and tossed his hands in the air. "Now what?"

Ethan shook his head and frowned. "I'm not sure, but I think you need to find out the truth before things get out of control."

The last thing Carter wanted was to confront Hannah. Maybe he'd taken things too fast. Maybe he should have been more cautious. He should have proceeded with caution while keeping his distance at the same time.

"I'd want to know the truth before I got too invested," Ethan said. "You know what I mean?"

"Yeah, I know what you're sayin'," Carter said, tossing the dirty rag into a nearby trash can on his way to the door. "I think it's already too late. And that's what I'm afraid of."

Carter stopped at the door and looked back at Ethan who was trailing right behind him. "You don't think that she commited a crime and is on the run, do you?"

Ethan lightly chuckled, but when Carter narrowed his eyes at him, he said, "It's hard to say, but she doesn't really seem like the type who would do something illegal."

Carter motioned for Ethan to go first and locked up the shop behind them on their way out. Carter would get to the bottom of it sooner rather than later, and on his own terms. If there was something Hannah was hiding, Carter wanted to be the first to know.

Chapter Seventeen

HANNAH LOOKED AT HER PHONE, SCROLLING through the messages she'd sent Carter over the last few days they'd been apart. She was still waiting for him to say something—anything. She'd thought about calling him, but knew that he would more than likely ignore that too.

She tried not to let it bother her. Tried harder not to take it personally. She knew that he had his hands full with Vince's vehicle, and, if the part had arrived between the last time she'd seen Carter and now, he would be fixing her car, too.

It wasn't like she was in a hurry for her car to get fixed now, anyway. The impending debt that she wouldn't be able to pay was mounting and, not to mention, the weatherman made more than one mention in the last few hours of an increasing threat of snow mixed with ice storm on its way to Maple Glen.

Hannah rocked Grace in her arms, finding comfort in her niece as she looked out the bedroom window. The silence of the early morning hours calmed Hannah's racing heart and eased her troubled mind.

She had woken an hour ago to Grace fussing in the crib. The sun had yet to peek over the horizon in the distance, but Hannah didn't mind waking up early. She had figured Grace would wake early due to falling asleep earlier than usual and sleeping through the night.

Now, the baby was zonked out and sawing logs in Hannah's arms.

Hannah swayed to a rhythm of her own as she allowed her mind to drift off. She thought of a way she could sneak out, put Maple Glen behind her and never look back. She hated that she didn't have enough money to cover the costs she had incurred, but then again, she wasn't a criminal either.

The only crime she'd ever committed in her lifetime was caring too much. Biting off more than she could chew and not knowing when to say enough was enough. Add being foolish to the list, too.

Shame on her for not thinking ahead. And shame on her for putting her trust in someone who wasn't one bit worthy of it.

The thought of her sister crossed her mind, and she couldn't help but worry about her. Hannah could be angry as all get out with her sister, but at the end of the day, Ashley was still her family. The only family she had left. And sure, Hannah chided herself for trusting Ashley and believing that everything was going well, but she still cared about her sister and what was going on back at home.

"Not home," she said aloud, wondering when she would finally realize that she didn't have a home. She'd lost it. The thought was never ending—revolving in her mind day after day, minute after minute. She needed to do something.

Hannah stepped back from the window when the smell of coffee wafted into the room. The smell of coffee signaled that Catie was awake and in the kitchen, so Hannah grabbed her phone.

She carefully laid Grace down in the crib, being sure not to make any sudden moves and jerk the baby awake. Hannah would use the time she had while Grace slept to talk to Catie about her predicament.

She laid the blanket over Grace, tucked it under the sleeping baby, and kissed her gently on the forehead. She loved the little girl more than anything else in the world. Her only hope was that it would be enough.

Taking her time, she carefully walked away from the crib and headed for the door. She stepped into the hallway and pulled the door closed behind her, leaving it open just a crack to be able to hear Grace when she woke.

Hannah tiptoed down the hallway, careful to avoid the squeaky spots in the floorboards as she made her way to the stairs. The smell of coffee got stronger the closer she got to the kitchen.

She wouldn't know what to do without coffee to kick start her mornings.

"Good mornin'," Catie greeted from the other side of the kitchen as Hannah walked in. Hannah feigned a smile, pretending that she hadn't been up for the last couple of hours contemplating a crime and how to get away with it.

"Coffee?" Catie asked, sliding a fresh-brewed cup of coffee across the counter as Hannah slid onto a chair. "How'd you sleep last night? I know that I could've slept better. Those winds are horrible out there."

Hannah nodded, taking a sip of her coffee and setting the cup back down in front of her. She played along with blaming her lack of sleep on the winds of the incoming storm. Not the thoughts of impending doom.

"The weatherman says we'll be getting up to five feet of snow by tonight," Catie said, sliding into a chair across from Hannah. Hannah's eyes widened in disbelief. "If we get that much snow, there's no way any of us are going anywhere for a while."

Catie's light chuckle danced around her eyes, and Hannah tried to laugh along with her, but it wasn't a laughing matter. Sure, she was perfectly fine in Maple Glen, but she didn't belong there.

"Even if Carter gets your car fixed, I'm not sure

you'll be able to leave once this storm hits," Catie said, her tone light and her voice a soft whisper.

"Well, he hasn't texted me back, so I'm not sure what the plan is," Hannah said, making no attempt to hide the frustration and disappointment in her voice. She hated that she'd set herself up like that. Depending on others was not something she liked to do. Falling head over heels for the man who was supposed to be fixing her car and who was now attempting to ghost her... that hadn't been in the plan either.

"I'm sure he's just busy with work," Catie assured her, taking a drink from her cup. "He gets involved in fixing cars, and it's almost like he vanishes into thin air sometimes."

Hannah nodded with a grin. She could believe it. Carter hadn't seemed like the type to take work less than seriously. That's what she liked about him. But unlike her, he seemed to have a good balance and wasn't all work and no play.

"Besides that, he likes you, Hannah," Catie said with a knowing smile. "And even if he didn't... he still needs money to keep his business runnin'."

Hannah faked a smile with a nervous chuckle. She wanted to say something along the lines of "yeah, about that," but instead, she kept quiet and stirred another splash of creamer into her coffee.

"Speaking of which," Catie said, glancing at the clock from the table they were sitting at. "I have to get Ethan up and headed that way soon. He told me last night that Vince was at the shop yesterday asking a thousand questions, wanting to know when his vehicle would be done."

Catie shook her head and rolled her eyes. "I'm sure Carter enjoyed that."

Hannah's heart raced at the thought of Vince asking questions. He hadn't seemed too impressed with her when he'd met her at the cabin. She couldn't help but wonder if the questions he asked were about Hannah rather than his vehicle.

"I'll be right back," Catie said as she stood from her chair and left the kitchen.

What if her sister had called the cops on her? What if she called her in for kidnapping Grace? The cops wouldn't know the truth, and they sure wouldn't take the time to listen to Hannah's side of the story once they found her with Grace in her arms, would they?

She took a deep breath and willed the thoughts away. She couldn't think about that right now.

Hannah grabbed her phone and tapped the screen. Still no missed calls or unread messages. She debated on whether to call Ashley. Her sister could just as easily have replied back to the messages Hannah had sent when she first arrived in Maple Glen.

Taking a deep breath, Hannah tapped the call button and waited for Ashley's voice on the other end of the line.

But instead, Hannah reached her voicemail and left an urgent message for her sister to call her back.

"It's important, Ash," she said as her voice shook with emotion.

She had wanted her sister to pick up. To answer the phone and let her know that she was okay. That everything was okay. She wanted to tell Ashley that Grace was okay. That she didn't want to take the baby, but she'd been left without a choice.

Warm tears streaked down Hannah's cheeks. Fear... frustration... worry... the emotions were uncontrollable.

Hannah could no longer pretend that she had everything together. Or even pretend that she was Grace's mother. Even if she liked it there in Maple Glen and had enjoyed her time while staying at the bed and breakfast.

She knew she could no longer go on pretending. No matter what happened, she needed to pull herself together and figure out what she was going to do. She needed to figure out what she was going to say.

She thought about Carter. She thought about what he would say or do when she would tell him the truth. Would he push her away, or would he pull her close and tell her that everything would be okay?

Hannah shook her head to clear the thoughts. Regardless of what Carter would do, she needed to do something because everything was falling apart, and it was only a matter of time before something terrible happened.

Chapter Eighteen

CARTER HAD PLANNED ON GOING TO CATIE'S bed and breakfast after work the other day, but instead, found himself avoiding the confrontation altogether. He felt bad about ignoring Hannah's messages, but he needed time to think things through.

He wasn't a man of many words, and he certainly wasn't in the position to call Hannah out on Vince's assumptions—no matter if he believed them or not. Carter was better than that. Even if the thought of Hannah running from trouble back home had crossed his mind several times in the last few days, it wouldn't do either of them any good if he crossed the line.

Instead, he would focus on fixing her car like he had first intended to do, now that the part had arrived and had been waiting for him on the shop's front step that morning. He would replace the alternator and give the car one more thorough look before turning it over to Hannah.

"Want some help with that?"

Carter turned around and was surprised to see Ethan standing in his garage. "Hey," he said, "I wasn't expecting you to show up today. I thought you'd be talkin' your gramps into retiring."

"You know just as well as I do that he isn't retiring anytime soon," Ethan said, a look of uncertainty crossing his face. Carter wasn't sure what was going on with the Davises but he knew how much Ethan wanted that hardware store. Other than Catie, the store had been the reason Ethan had decided to stay in Maple Glen. "I think he was just full of it and in on your aunt's matchmaking scheme when he mentioned giving the store to me."

Carter let out a laugh and nodded. "Maybe. It's hard to say for sure what those ol' coots are up to nowadays."

Ethan approached the work bench and grabbed the unopened package housing the alternator. He held it up and raised a brow at Carter. "Is this what I think it is?"

Carter took a step toward him, grunting as he snatched the box out of his hands. "It is, but unlike what you're thinkin', it just got here this morning and I haven't had time to get it out yet."

Ethan slid onto a nearby barstool and leaned against the closest toolbox. When Carter shot him a sharp glare, Ethan held up his hands and said, "Take it easy, man. I believe ya."

Carter pulled up a chair next to Ethan and was wondering how much work would actually get done with the two of them sitting around and killing time. He grabbed his coffee from the toolbox behind him and took a drink.

"I thought you were going to confront her about everything, anyway," Ethan said, shoving his keys into the front pocket of his jeans and sitting back down. Carter watched his movement from the corner of his eye as he thought of a good enough answer. "Have you talked to her about it?"

Carter gripped the steel mug in his hands as he thought about it. "Nah, not yet."

Ethan shook his head and leaned his shoulder into the corner of Carter's toolbox. "Time's running out," he said. "You and I both know that once her car is fixed, she's out of here."

Carter bit his tongue, willing the urge to knock Ethan off of his stool to pass as he looked straight ahead and gripped his coffee mug tighter. He didn't need a reminder that she was leaving. He needed the reminder as much as he needed Vince in his shop asking questions while making assumptions. Neither of the two were helping Carter figure things out.

"Yeah," Carter said, sliding off his seat and setting his mug down. "Then I guess I better stop wasting time and get her car fixed so she can get out of here, huh?"

Ethan sat back with eyes wide as Carter grabbed the alternator out of the box and made his way over to Hannah's car. He couldn't hide his frustration with the situation any longer. He didn't want to lose his cool over something as unreasonable as miscommunication and misguided assumptions, but it was proving to be a challenge.

Carter didn't regret a lot of things, but there was some regret with getting involved with a woman he hardly knew. As far as he knew, she was blowing smoke and pretending to be someone that she wasn't. She could very easily be exactly who Vince was implying she was and could lead Carter astray.

It wouldn't be the first time a woman set Carter up just to let him down.

"Hey, man," Ethan said, following him to the car. "I didn't mean to upset you. I know you've got a lot going on and you've gotten attached to some kind of ideal life with Hannah and Grace, but—"

"Yeah, well..." Carter popped the hood of the car open and moved around Ethan who was now standing next to the driver's side of the car. He pried the hood open and propped a two-by-four in place to keep it from closing on him while he worked. "I guess I'll have to figure everything out on my own, then, won't I?"

Ethan took a step back, most likely afraid that Carter would come out from under the hood any given minute and start swinging. Carter was riled up. He'd give him that. But he wouldn't go rounds with Ethan about it. It wasn't worth it.

"Honestly," Carter said, taking his tone down a notch, "I can't wrap my head around everything Vince is thinking. She doesn't seem like the type who would be running from the law."

When Ethan didn't answer, Carter furrowed a brow and took a step back from the car. "I mean, think about it. She has a baby with her. Who in their right mind would break the law and throw a baby into the middle of it?"

Ethan slowly nodded and Carter wondered if he was on the same page as him. "Let's just get her car fixed, and I'll figure everything out later."

Ethan grabbed a set of tools and made his way over to the front of the car. They would work together and fix Hannah's car. Once the car was fixed, Carter would call her and tell her that she could come and get it.

Maybe by then he would have a plan of action in mind and would hopefully be able to find out the truth without causing any more problems—for either of them.

Chapter Nineteen

HANNAH LEANED AGAINST THE KITCHEN counter and watched the snow fall to the ground. It had accumulated over the last few hours, and the winds hadn't died down yet. According to the weatherman on TV, they should expect to see strong winds, sleet, and snow over the course of the next three days.

Hannah sighed. It was just beginning.

She pushed away from the counter and made her way out of the kitchen and into the living room where Alex and Grace were both being entertained by Catie. Hannah smiled at the sight before her as she took a seat in the recliner. Grace's eyes watched Catie's sock-covered hands as she sprawled out on a patchwork quilt that Hannah had found in the room upstairs.

"What do you think his name should be?" Catie asked, pretending the socks on her hands were puppets and giving them a life of their own while keeping Alex rolling in a fit of laughter. Hannah couldn't help but laugh along with Alex. Catie was a hoot, and the Sharpie-drawn faces on the socks were perfectly fitting for the show she was putting on.

"Alvin!" Alex shouted and clapped as she sat in front of Catie on her knees. "Alvin and Fred!"

"Alright then," Catie said with a silent laugh, "Alvin, what do you think we should do today?"

Hannah chuckled as Catie exchanged conversation between the two socks on her hands, all while Duke was trying to get a hold of them and rip them away from her. "No, Duke," Catie hollered, but it was no use. Hannah watched in excitement as Duke snatched Alvin and shot out of the room. Hannah laughed out loud as Catie chased after the dog. She wondered if there would ever be a dull moment at the bed and breakfast, but soon decided that as long as Duke was still young and the kids were able to play, Catie would have her hands full and Hannah wouldn't have to worry about being bored.

The thought of leaving crossed her mind as she watched the show unravel in front of her. The fireplace crackled and popped as the wood gave in to the flames. She found comfort at the bed and breakfast. Not only there, but with Maple Glen in general.

She didn't have a clue what she would do once her car was fixed. She had texted Tara and let her know that her next move was still up in the air. Especially since she'd had to wait so long for her car to get fixed.

Though, truthfully, that didn't matter so much as she was secretly waiting for her sister to call her.

She still held out hope for Ashley to respond to the missed calls and messages that Hannah had left for her. It was only a matter of time before Ashley gave in and called Hannah. Hannah knew that her sister had a problem, but she also knew that Ashley had a heart. That she cared whether she chose to show it or not.

Hannah wiped a stray tear from her cheek as Alex looked over at her. "What's wrong, Hannah?"

Hannah smiled through the tears and uncertainty. The thought of something happening to Ashley had crossed Hannah's mind too many times to count. If something happened to Ashley, she would never forgive herself for leaving Chicago.

Alex patted Hannah's arm and asked, "Why are you crying? Are you okay?"

The little girl climbed onto Hannah's lap and wrapped her arms around her neck. "Oh, honey, I'm okay," she said, trying her hardest to keep her emotions under control while talking to Alex. She felt bad that she'd caught the girl's attention in the first place, distracting her from having fun with Catie and Duke. "I just miss my sister, is all."

"Your car will be fixed soon, and then you can go and see her," Alex said, patting Hannah on the back before climbing off of her lap.

Hannah watched as Alex went back to playing on the floor with Grace. The little girl was right. Once her car was fixed, Hannah could go and see her sister. The only problem was that she didn't know where to find her.

She'd tried to find her before packing up what little they'd had and leaving with Grace. She looked high and low and spent hours tracking Ashley down. The only thing she could have done differently was to report her as a missing person, but she knew from the past few times Ashley had done something like this, the police didn't see it like that. They figured Ashley was an adult and willingly set out of her own accord and was safe—no matter how many times Hannah tried to tell them that her sister might be in trouble and needed their help finding her.

Her thoughts were interrupted by the ringing of her phone. She shot out of the chair, knowing it could be just about anyone, but she silently prayed for it to be Ashley. She needed to hear her voice. She needed to hear that she was okay and that she was alive.

She didn't care that her sister had abandoned them. She only cared that she was okay.

Hannah raced to the phone and was a mix of emotions as she stared at the number on the screen.

Carter.

She debated for a split second on whether or not to answer his call. He had, in fact, avoided her messages for the better part of the last week. She wouldn't admit that having him ignore her hurt, and she certainly wouldn't allow him to justify hurting her by saying he had work to do.

She angrily swiped the red x with her thumb and took a deep breath. She needed to get a hold of her emotions before she lost it.

"Everything okay?" Catie asked, rounding the corner of the hallway and entering the living room. Hannah glanced down at her phone and looked back at Catie. "Yeah, wrong number, is all," she bluffed, shoving her phone into her back pocket before making her way over to Grace.

"Are you sure?"

Catie's question broke Hannah's resolve just as her phone vibrated.

Ignoring Catie's question for now, Hannah pulled the phone from her pocket and read a message from Carter.

Your car is ready.

"Perfect," Hannah said, tapping her thumbs along the keyboard and sending a reply back to him. A simple thank you would have to do until she was face to face with him. Until then, she needed to get her thoughts straight and her emotions in check.

CATIE HAD VOLUNTEERED ETHAN TO GIVE Hannah a ride to Carter's shop to get her car while looking after Grace. There was something about the way Catie looked at her that told Hannah that she knew there was something bothering her.

Hannah thought about telling Catie before leaving the house with Ethan, but decided against it. She would get her car from Carter, pay him what she could and hope that by morning she would be on her way with Grace. Either to Chicago to find her sister or to Tara's, it was yet to be determined.

"Thanks for the ride," she said, climbing out of Ethan's truck once they arrived at Carter's shop. She was thankful that Catie and Ethan had been so willing to help her out since day one. If it weren't for them, she wasn't sure what she would have done.

She flung the strap of her purse over her shoulder and walked inside, wishing what happened between her and Carter never would have, now that things had turned awkward between them.

The bell above the door announced her arrival, and she caught Carter's eyes staring at her from behind the counter before she was even ten steps inside. The magnetic pull she'd felt with him was still there, buzzing wildly between them. She hated that she'd let her guard down and allowed him to have that effect on her.

She hated it even more that she allowed him to hurt her when she had least expected it.

"Hey," he said, making his way around the counter. "I take it you got my message."

"Which one?" she asked sarcastically, shooting him

a withering glare. "You've sent so many I'm not sure which one you're referring to."

"Hannah, look," he said, taking a step toward her. She took a step back, willing him to keep his distance. He stopped in his tracks and held his hand out. "I can explain why I haven't—"

"There's no need to explain," she said, fumbling for her purse. "Just tell me how much I owe you, and once I pay you, I'll be gone so you don't have to see me again."

"Hannah, stop," he said, stepping toward her once again and closing the distance between them. Her eyes filled with tears as she prayed for them not to fall. "Hannah..."

The desperation in his voice caught her attention, willing her to look at him as the scent of his cologne clung to air she inhaled through her nose. She pulled her wallet from her purse. "I mean it, Carter. Just tell me how much I owe you, and I'll be out of town by morning."

He grabbed a hold of her arms, forcing her to look at him. She looked into his eyes, and she could see a storm brewing inside of them. "I'm sorry," he said, "I didn't mean to ignore your messages. I got caught up with everything goin' on that I—"

"Don't," she said with a jerk of her body, forcing him to release his hands from her arms. She didn't need to hear excuses. She'd heard enough of those in her past to last her a lifetime. "I don't care. And it doesn't matter, anyway."

"Yes, you do," Carter said, staring her in the eyes with a sincerity she had never witnessed before today. "And yes, it does matter."

She challenged him with a raised brow as she crossed her arms over her chest. "What do you want from me, Carter?"

She was hurt. She had been stranded in a town she didn't know in the middle of nowhere, several hours from the place she had once called home, fallen for a man who had come to her rescue, and now... Now none of it mattered, and she should have known that nothing good lasts forever.

"The truth," he said, exhaling his words on a sigh.

She took a step back. "The truth?"

He narrowed his eyes, and she knew that he knew. Maybe he didn't know everything, but there was something he knew that she hadn't told him. The thought of Vince flashed in her mind, rousing her suspicions that the guy didn't like her.

"Is that why you quit responding to my messages?" she asked, not only wanting to know what Carter was thinking, but why.

"No."

She shook her head. "Yes, it is. Instead of asking me if what you've heard about me is true, you avoided me like the plague instead. Leaving me hanging and wondering why I even spent time with you. Why I even took the time to get to know you."

Carter took a step back like her words had pierced him. "Don't say that," he said as his eyes narrowed. She didn't care if she hurt him. The way he'd ignored her had hurt, and right now, all that mattered was that her car was fixed. She had told herself that she wasn't going to stoop to the level of fighting over miscommunication and avoidance. She was better than that.

"Then tell me why you refused to talk to me. Why you ghosted me," she pleaded, stepping closer to him to make her point that he had hurt her. She had too much going on to deal with this too. "What did Vince say that made you think twice and change your mind about me?"

His jaw dropped at the mention of Vince, and she knew that she was spot on with her assumptions that Vince didn't like her. She knew it from the minute they'd met at the cabin. There was something telling in the way he had looked at her that day—like he was trying to figure out what she was trying to keep a secret.

Regardless of whether or not she was keeping secrets was her business, and she could only imagine that Vince was thinking like *only* a cop would. Which meant that he had Carter believing that she was a criminal.

"I'm not a criminal," she said, her voice cracking with emotion as she said the words. She chastised herself for allowing the emotion to break through. She didn't want to cry, but the necessity of admitting that she wasn't a criminal to the man she had felt a connection with broke her heart.

"Hannah, I didn't—"

"I'm homeless."

She said the words loud and clear. It was just the two of them in the shop, and if she was going to tell the truth, she wanted it to be right then and there. No more second guessing herself or wondering what Carter would say or do. It was now or never.

She had wanted to tell Carter the truth since the day they'd gotten closer, but for some unknown reason, she had refused to allow herself the freedom to release the burden.

"Homeless?" There was a fierceness in his tone, and she could see the torment in his eyes. He cared. It was written all over his face.

"Yes, homeless," she replied, keeping her eyes on her hands as she was nervously wringing them in front of her. She hated admitting that she'd lost everything... that she'd trusted the wrong person... "And Grace isn't mine."

The words were out of her mouth within seconds, and in an instant she regretted saying them so quickly without giving Carter time to process. He stepped back as if she had slapped him across the face. "What?"

"I know," she said, tears streaming down her face and messing up more than just her makeup. When she saw him reach for his phone, she reached out for his hand and stopped him. "No, don't. I don't need the law involved. I'm not a kidnapper, I promise."

He looked down at his phone, debating on whether to take her word for it or not, but finally set it down on a faded red toolbox next to them. He ran a hand through his hair and gripped the back of his neck. Conflicted by the information she had just laid on him. She couldn't blame him, but at least now he knew the truth. "My—"

"Wait," he held up a hand in front of him, pausing her from further explaining the mess of a situation she'd gotten herself into. "If you're not Grace's mother, then who—"

"My sister."

He looked her in the eye. "Your sister? What happened to your sister? Why do you have her daughter?"

She swiped at the tears on her face and tried to explain it to him. "I don't know," she choked out. Emotions she had bottled up and shoved down deep inside of her bubbled to the surface and threatened to escape as she stared into Carter's eyes. She wanted him to know everything. She wouldn't blame him for hating her after hearing everything, but at the same time, she just wanted him to hold her. To tell her that everything would be okay whether she believed it or not.

"What do you mean you don't know," Carter said,

his tone sharp and edged with emotion of his own. He reached for his phone again, ran a thumb against the screen and threatened, "Maybe I should call Vince. This sounds like somethin' he should be involved with."

She cried out and begged him not to involve Vince. She didn't need him involved in it. She did nothing wrong. But then again, maybe if Vince got involved, maybe the city cops would take her complaints of Ashley missing more seriously. "She's gone."

"She died?" he asked, setting the phone aside once again before running his hand through his hair once more. "This just keeps getting better and better."

"She's an addict. She left Grace alone in the apartment," she sputtered out, tears streaming harder and faster down her face. "I came home from... I came home, and Grace was there by herself with an eviction notice on the door."

Carter brushed his thumb across her cheek, wiping away the fallen tears with a gentleness she'd only experienced with him. "Hannah, I'm—"

She cried out, allowing the tears to fall harder as she cried for her sister. For Grace. And for herself. "I had no choice but to take Grace and leave. I wanted to get to Tara's as fast as I could..."

"Shhh... it's okay," he said, bringing her in close to him and wrapping his strong arms around her. He kissed the top of her forehead and held her tightly against him. She could hear the racing of his heart as it beat wildly inside his chest.

She couldn't believe she'd let it all out. That she told him everything she'd been holding back.

"I'm just trying to find somewhere to go," she whimpered against his chest, feeling her own heart break from the honesty of her words. "A place to call home and take care of Grace."

He rubbed her back, and she felt safe in his arms. He had been upset with her just moments ago, but not now, and she thanked God for that. "Shh, it's okay. You're safe here. I've got you."

She pressed herself into his chest and allowed his strong arms to comfort her. She needed him now more than ever, and it didn't matter how vulnerable she was at the moment. She trusted him to help her get through it.

"It's going to be okay," he said, kissing her on the top of her head. "I'll take care of you and Grace. And as long as you're here, you've got a home, Hannah."

Chapter Twenty

HE WASN'T SURE WHAT HE WAS GOING TO DO with the information Hannah had told him, but one thing he was sure of—he was going to do whatever it took to take care of her and Grace. He was foolish and reckless for getting himself involved with her—whether she left town in the morning or never left at all—but he didn't regret it. He would never regret it.

He had ended the night with her in his arms, holding her tightly against his chest while promising to take care of her and Grace. She had mentioned leaving town in the morning, and regardless of how many times he told her that she didn't have to leave, she still felt it was necessary.

He'd gone home with an uneasy feeling in the pit of his stomach, knowing that by morning, Hannah and Grace would be gone. Out of his life faster than they'd entered it. The worst part about the realization was that there wasn't a single thing he could do to stop Hannah from leaving.

Just like the last woman he'd given his heart to. Nothing would stop a woman from leaving if leaving was the only thing on their mind.

He woke to the thought of Hannah leaving town without so much as a goodbye or a see you later, and it nearly killed him. He'd called Vince and explained what Hannah had told him. Not because Hannah told him not to, but because her sister was still in the city of Chicago without anyone looking for her. Hannah was upset at her sister for what she'd done, but mostly she was scared. He'd seen the way she cringed at the mention of where Ashley could be.

Carter had Vince's word that he would take care of it and make sure they found Ashley. Carter trusted that Vince wouldn't stop until the city cops gave him what he wanted—even if Vince had to go to Chicago himself, Ashley would be found.

Carter glanced down at his phone and crawled out of bed. No messages or missed calls, and that alone worried him. Hannah could have left town in the middle of the night with Grace just like she'd done in Chicago—in the middle of another snowstorm.

He sent her a message, hoping that she would respond back to him.

He needed to get to the shop and work on the

other vehicles, but he would keep his phone close while waiting for Hannah to message him back while he prayed like crazy that she hadn't left town.

Chapter Twenty-One

IT SHOULD HAVE BEEN EASY TO PACK UP THEIR things and leave. She stared at the message on the screen from Carter. A simple hello. Of course, she knew that he was just checking in. Checking to see if she had left Maple Glen yet, or if she was sticking around.

She had thought about what she was going to do come morning, but had fallen asleep before coming up with an answer. She knew she couldn't leave. Not when the temperatures were barely above freezing and the snow was blowing like crazy.

Even when she left Carter's shop, she was a nervous wreck on the drive back to the bed and break-fast. The snow had fallen relentlessly overnight, and from what she could see out of her bedroom window, it wouldn't be too much longer before people would have to dig their way out if they wanted to go anywhere.

Hannah's phone pinged and vibrated in her hand. She'd been staring mindlessly out the window while trying to come up with a plan of action. She could stay in town and continue pretending that she lived in a Hallmark movie. Or she could brave the weather and head out of town without looking back.

She thought about calling Tara. She would be able to tell her everything and, together, they would come up with a brilliant idea. Whether Tara told her to stay put or not, Hannah had only one way to find out.

She scrolled through her contacts and was prepared to call Tara until a text message from an unknown number appeared on the screen.

Han it's Ash. Come back home please

A jolt of adrenaline shot through Hannah causing her to jump to her feet from the edge of the bed she'd been sitting on for the last hour. Before she realized what she was doing, her fingers were flying across the letters on the bottom of her screen.

Was it really Ashley who was texting her? What happened to her sister's phone?

Hannah took a deep breath, willing her sister to respond to her messages. The seconds turned to minutes, and Hannah couldn't take it any longer.

Pressing the call button, she pressed the phone to her ear and waited for Ashley to pick up on the other end. She had no time to think about what she would say or do if it wasn't Ashley who answered. She just needed to know for sure.

"Han, where are you? Do you have Grace?"

A sharp cry escaped Hannah's lips as she heard Ashley's voice on the other end of the line. "Ash..." she choked, trying her best to keep it together. "Where have you been? Where'd you go?"

"Please say you have my daughter, please."

The panic she heard in Ashley's voice paled in comparison to the fear Hannah had felt over the last few weeks. If Ashley had been truly worried about her daughter, why hadn't she called sooner?

"Yes, I have Grace. Now, tell me where you are and what's going on," Hannah demanded in a sharp tone. She'd had enough with not knowing the answers to her questions.

"Please just come home," Ashley begged, emotion cracked her voice. "Please, Han. I'll explain everything if you just come home."

Hannah thought about the home she had left. The home that no longer existed because of unfair circumstances due to her sister's actions. It wasn't fair that her sister had left without a care in the world, shattering the security they'd had, yet now she was begging for Hannah to put the pieces back together.

"What happened to your phone? I've been texting and calling you nonstop since you left," Hannah asked, keeping her voice down in a harsh whisper. She glanced over at the crib where Grace was wrapped in a blanket fast asleep. "You left us..."

Hannah let her words trail off. The emotional rollercoaster she was on was at its all time low as everything came crashing down.

"I'm sorry, Han. I can explain. Just come home, and we can work it out."

Hannah shook her head. She wasn't going anywhere. "What do you mean, home? That place doesn't exist anymore, Ash."

The trembling of her bottom lip distracted her from saying anything else. The last thing she needed was to allow her emotions to take control of the conversation. Hannah still needed to know where Ashley was and if she was okay. Whether or not Ashley would tell her was yet to be determined.

"Ash," she called out. She heard a man talking in the background, but she couldn't hear what was being said. "Ashley. Answer me."

"I'm here," her sister answered. "Tell me where you are, and I'll come to you."

Hannah sighed as she rolled her eyes. For whatever reason, her sister was unwilling to give Hannah the information she was wanting to know. She couldn't determine if Ashley just didn't want to tell Hannah, or if her surroundings were holding her back from being able to tell.

Instead of wasting more time, Hannah said, "I'm

in a small town called Maple Glen. It's about three hours from Chicago."

When Ashley didn't say anything, Hannah said, "Tell me where you are, and I'll come get you."

"Don't worry, Han. I'll find a way there," Ashley said. Her words were spoken in a rush as the man in the background demanded his phone back. "I've got to go, but I'll see you soon."

The click echoed in Hannah's ear, and she immediately felt disconnected from Ashley. Her heart sank at knowing her sister was out there, alive but alone, among people who were impatient and uncaring.

"Hey, is everything alright?" Catie asked as she leaned against the bedroom doorway. "I wasn't trying to eavesdrop or anything, I just came up here because I heard you talking and—"

"It's not," Hannah sputtered, wiping angrily at the fresh tears streaming down her cheeks. She wasn't a crier. The last thing she wanted to do was cry when her sister needed her. "My sister... she's..."

Catie entered the bedroom, walking straight to Hannah and wrapping her in a hug. Catie guided Hannah to the bed and sat down beside her. Hannah didn't want to sit and talk about it. She needed to go. She needed to get to Chicago and find Ashley.

The thought of calling Carter crossed her mind, but there was nothing he could do that she wasn't already doing herself. She pulled away from Catie and pushed herself away from the bed. She kept her voice low, afraid of waking Grace.

Hannah didn't need the little one awake and scared from the intense emotions racing through her. "I need to call the cops. They need to find Ashley," she said, running shaking hands through her hair as she tried to think of her next move. Catie stood up and walked toward her. "Do you want me to call Vince? I'm not sure what's going on, but if you need the police..."

Hannah choked back a sob as she nodded. She hated that she was relying on a man who had misjudged her, but right now, it didn't matter. She pushed all of that aside and focused on the here and now.

"Okay," Catie said, glancing over her shoulder at Grace, who was still asleep in the crib behind them. Catie reached for Hannah's hand and guided her into the hallway and toward the stairs. "Let's go downstairs and figure everything out."

The look of concern etched on Catie's face told Hannah that she had a lot of explaining to do. There wasn't enough time to explain. Ashley needed her.

ONCE CATIE PLACED THE CALL, IT HADN'T taken Vince long to show up at the house. And once he got enough information about Ashley and her possible whereabouts while encouraging Hannah to stay put, he was gone again.

Hannah sat across from Catie at the kitchen counter. Catie's eyes filled with worry as they stared back at Hannah.

"Everything will be okay," Catie said, trying her best to comfort Hannah. Hannah nodded while taking a deep breath. No matter how many times she'd heard it, she knew that it wasn't guaranteed. "Vince will stop at nothing to find her. Even if that means going to the city and looking for her himself."

Hannah nodded, knowing that to be true about Vince. Carter had said the same about the Chief Deputy.

"I didn't want this to happen," Hannah said, tracing a thumb around the top of her coffee cup. Thoughts of her sister being alone in the big city by herself and surrounded by people who didn't care about her like Hannah did made Hannah's heart break. She hated herself for leaving Chicago the way that she had. If only she had stuck around for a little while longer, Ashley would be with her, and Hannah wouldn't be worried for her safety. "I should have never left Chicago."

Catie sat quietly on the opposite side of the counter as she listened to Hannah tell all. Hannah had wanted to tell Catie the truth long before now. She felt bad for pretending to be someone she wasn't. Even if it was for her own good at the time.

"You can't blame yourself," Catie said, locking her eyes on Hannah's and taking a drink of her coffee. "I don't know the whole story. Only bits and pieces from what you told Vince... but I know for a fact that you did what you thought was best for Grace."

Hannah nodded. Everything she had done—from leaving their apartment in Chicago to taking the last minute trip to Tara's—had been for the sake of Grace and making sure she would be okay.

"That speaks volumes in and of itself, Hannah," Catie said, trying her best to assure Hannah that she hadn't done anything wrong. "If it had been one of my sisters and I were in your shoes, I can't say that I would have done anything different."

Hannah felt comforted by Catie's words. She thought about Ashley and how upset she was about Hannah leaving Chicago. She hadn't had time to explain over the phone to her sister that it was for the best and she wanted to protect Grace. Aside from the fact that they were homeless, Hannah was trying to do the best she could with what little she had.

"I just hope that once they find her, she doesn't hate me," Hannah whispered, wiping tears away with a worn out napkin. "It was just the three of us. I looked everywhere for her when I came home. I was so shocked when I found Grace laying in her crib."

A sob escaped, leaving Hannah feeling more and more vulnerable as she recalled the harsh memories. "At first, I thought she had just ran to the neighbor's apartment for milk or something. But time went by and she didn't come home... and knowing that we'd had a fight the day before..."

"Vince and the city cops will find her," Catie said, sliding off her chair and making her way over to Hannah before wrapping her arms around her. "Everything is going to be okay."

Hannah nodded, taking in the reassurance and allowing it to sink in. Her phone vibrated against the counter in front of her, and her heart jolted. She swiped it off the counter and opened the message without missing a beat.

I'm on my way to you.

Chapter Twenty-Two

TIME HAD GOTTEN AWAY FROM HIM, AND before he knew it, he had gone all day without checking his phone.

He lifted it from the faded toolbox and unlocked it with a quick swipe of his thumb.

Still no message from Hannah. He couldn't help but feel at a loss for words when he opened a new message and stared at the blinking cursor.

He thought twice about sending her a message. But if she had wanted to talk to him, she would have replied to the message he'd sent earlier that morning.

Knowing his luck with women, she was long gone with everything behind her.

He kicked himself for fixing her car. He had given her an out without hesitating. Not to mention the weather. That alone should have kept her in town.

Carter flipped the shop's light off and grabbed his

truck keys. He needed to head home and grab a bite to eat, even though stopping by Charlie's bar sounded better yet.

Carter nodded at the thought. That was exactly what he was going to do. Besides, it had been a while since he'd had a chat with Charlie.

Ever since his brother fell in love with Autumn, Carter had a hard time catching his brother by himself.

He chuckled at his previous belief that it'd never happen to him. Falling for his aunt's antics of match-making and falling in love so easily.

Finding love in a small town was difficult...

Or at least, it had been until Hannah came along.

He stepped outside, instantly wishing he had remembered his stocking cap and gloves as the winter's harsh winds hit his face.

Carter fumbled the key into the ignition and fired up his truck before grabbing the ice scraper from the floorboard.

He hated winter. He hated the cold, period. But he loved Maple Glen, and if living in a town he enjoyed and successfully ran a business in while living close to his family meant he had to deal with the cold, brutal winter months, so be it.

After scraping the ice from his windshield, he climbed back into the driver's seat of his truck and headed out of the parking lot.

Knowing that his brother would offer him a cold one on the house, along with a bite to eat, Carter guided his truck along the back roads to the other side of town where his brother's bar was located.

"Whoa," Charlie called out. "Do I know you?"

Carter laughed, taking hold of his brother's hand and giving it a quick shake before pulling him in for a brotherly hug. "It's been awhile, but not *that* long."

Charlie flipped a rag over his shoulder and said, "Whatever you say. Now, what can I get ya?"

Carter wanted the usual, and that's what his brother gave him. Nothing spectacular. Just a cold bottle of beer. Enough to take the edge off and allow Carter to relax while enjoying his visit with Charlie.

"So, how are things with Autumn?"

He held the neck of the bottle between two fingers and swung it back and forth. He didn't care to hear about his brother's almost-too-perfect relationship with the wedding planner and Cara's best friend, but it was just enough small talk to keep his mind off of Hannah.

"It's goin' great, actually," Charlie said, beaming. "She said yes when I popped the question."

Charlie waggled his eyebrows and Carter chucked the bottle cap at him. "Get out of here. You're not engaged. There's no way someone would want to marry you."

Carter shook his head and tipped the bottle back.

Charlie offered an innocent shrug and said, "It won't be long until she's plannin' our wedding."

Carter set the bottle down in front of him and shook his head once again. He still couldn't believe that his siblings had fallen into Fran's trap.

"How about you? What's goin' on with you and Hannah?"

Carter tipped his head back and laughed. "Word travels fast, huh?"

Charlie shrugged and wiped up a wet spot on the counter between them. "Small town. Not much else to say about that, Car."

Carter tipped the bottle up and drank the last swallow. He set the empty down and asked for another. He didn't want to get too sloshed, but he wanted to feel good, and one wasn't going to cut it.

"So I heard she was leaving town as soon as her car was fixed," Charlie said. "Have you fixed it yet? I'm sure you're takin' your time on it, right?"

Charlie chuckled as he reached across the counter and nudged Carter's arm with his fist.

"Finished it yesterday," Carter admitted, popping the top off the second bottle of beer that Charlie slid in front of him.

Charlie quirked a brow. "That doesn't sound good."

Carter shot a glance in the direction of the dart board. He looked back at Charlie and hooked a thumb over his shoulder and asked, "How 'bout a game of darts?"

Charlie set the rag he'd been holding on the counter and nodded as he met Carter in front of the dart board. "Best of three?"

"Whatever works," Carter said, grabbing the darts from his brother's hand.

"She leave town already, then?" Charlie asked, standing behind Carter.

Carter flicked his wrist and sent the dart sailing toward the board. He was out of practice and it showed as the dart bounced off the board and landed at his feet.

"Whoa, easy there, killer," Charlie teased, slapping a hand on Carter's back. "Relax. You're too tense, bro."

Carter shrugged his brother off and took another shot at the bullseye. *Missed again.*

"Easier said than done," he mumbled.

"I take it you two had a falling out or somethin'? She leave town without looking back?"

Carter knew his brother was only trying to strike up a conversation. The same reason Carter had decided to stop by the bar. He missed having conversations with his brothers. The visit had been long overdue.

"Something like that," Carter said, tossing his third dart at the board and grunting when it bounced off the edge.

"Wanna talk about it?"

Carter shrugged as he headed toward the board. He grabbed the darts and walked back to Charlie.

Throwing darts had been a thing to do when his brothers had spent time together. If he had it his way, he and his siblings would visit more often than they had in the last few months.

He knew that he'd buried himself in work at the shop, and he also knew that finding free time while matching up schedules was easier said than done. An ongoing theme for the night.

"It depends," Carter finally answered. "How much do you know?"

Charlie shot him a knowing grin, and Carter shook his head.

"Small town, remember?"

"I didn't plan on getting involved with her," Carter admitted, taking hold of the darts and toeing the line. He aimed and fired a dart at the board. To his surprise, it hooked dead center. *Bullseye.*

"That's usually how it happens," Charlie said with a light chuckle. "It happens when we least expect it. At least, that's my story and I'm stickin' to it."

Carter laughed and took a quick sip from the bottle. "I don't know. There was just something about her... and Grace."

He thought of the baby, and an ache caused him to tighten his grip on the bottle.

"I can't believe she left in the snowstorm," Charlie said, taking a shot at winning points at the board. "I haven't been out there yet, but from the sounds of it, it's getting pretty bad."

Carter tossed back the last of his beer and set the empty on a nearby table. He didn't want to think about the weather and Hannah driving in it with Grace right along with her.

He slid his phone out of his back pocket. If he was lucky, Hannah would text him and at least let him know that they made it to wherever they were headed.

A part of him wondered why he hadn't pushed harder to make her stay. Why he'd given up so easily and accepted it for what it was.

If anything happened to them, he would never forgive himself for letting them leave without a fight.

Chapter Twenty-Three

ASHLEY WAS ON HER WAY TO MAPLE GLEN.

The thought alone excited Hannah, but also caused an unsettled feeling in the pit of her stomach.

Of course, Hannah had texted her back with the address to the bed and breakfast. And of course, once Ashley arrived at the house, their reunion would be witnessed by Catie and whoever else was there unexpectedly.

That alone caused Hannah's heart to beat at an unnatural rate while she swore she'd have a panic attack any minute.

Hannah had called Tara to fill her in and unfortunately cancel their plans of getting together.

She couldn't leave now even if she wanted to. With the blizzard and now her sister arriving... and she couldn't forget about Carter.

She glanced down at her phone and debated on

whether or not to tell him that not only was she staying, but that her sister was coming too.

Just as she was preparing to send him a quick update, she heard heavy footsteps on the front porch.

She glanced over her shoulder, checking to see where Catie was and if she was nearby. She was nowhere to be seen, but Hannah could hear her in the kitchen with the girls as she prepared lunch for Alex.

Hannah made her way to the front door, hesitant to get too close. She was half tempted to run and hide because she didn't think she was ready for what awaited her on the other side of the door.

A soft knock rattled the door's oval window and Hannah held her breath as the knob turned.

Vince pushed open the door and stepped inside. Hannah took a step back and kept her distance.

She had a feeling that Ashley would be a mix of emotions. Which meant there was no telling what would happen in the next few minutes.

Hannah just prayed that everything would go smoothly and Ashley would follow through with a decent conversation.

"Is she with you?" Hannah asked, looking behind Vince for any sign of her sister. Vince nodded with a sympathetic look on his face. Hannah didn't doubt it was a difficult task to be an officer. Let alone taking it upon oneself to search for someone out of their jurisdiction.

He stepped to the side and allowed Hannah to get

a good look at her older sister. Her only sister. Her family—in fact, the only family she had left aside from Grace.

"Ash." Hannah choked back a sob, raising her hand to her mouth in an attempt to hide her shock. Her sister stood beside Vince with an unreadable expression on her face. Her hair was ratted and snarled in braids, and the clothes she wore were disheveled.

Ashley stared at Hannah in silence, and in that moment, Hannah saw tears welling in her sister's eyes.

"Ash, come here," Hannah said, holding her arms out as she walked up to her sister. "I'm so glad you're okay."

She stepped back, getting a good look up close and personal of her sister before asking, "You're okay?"

Tears burned Hannah's eyes as she took in her sister's uncertainty in the matter. Vince stepped off to the side and mentioned giving them a few minutes alone before having the dreaded conversation—what to do with Ashley now that she was there.

Hannah knew that her sister needed help. There was no doubt about that. But first, she needed to make sure she understood why Hannah did what she did and that she still loved her no matter what happened.

She heard Vince tell Catie that Ashley was there. Hannah knew that it was taking a lot of effort for Catie not to make her way into the front entrance and welcome Ashley inside.

Hannah loved Catie's hospitality and the way she

made everyone feel welcome—especially the way she'd made Hannah feel right at home in her moment of need.

"Han, I need help."

Ashley's words caught Hannah off guard. She hadn't expected her sister to come right out and admit she had a problem. Even though that's the first thing they'd learned when she attended Ashley's first alcoholics anonymous family group with her last year. The year Hannah realized that her sister had a problem with alcohol and needed help.

"We'll get you help as soon as we can, okay?" Hannah wasn't sure what the roads were like from the small town to a nearby hospital, but she was certain they'd be able to get Ashley help no matter what.

"Can I see her?"

Hannah choked back another sob. Her sister wanted to see her baby. The same baby that she'd left at the apartment all alone and without a mother.

"Grace?"

Hannah's question was one that requested an obvious response. Ashley nodded her head and glanced around the room.

"She's in the kitchen with Catie," Hannah said, hooking a thumb over her shoulder while trying to keep her emotions in check. She didn't want to cry and get all emotional when Ashley needed someone to be strong for her. Ashley needed Hannah now more than ever, and Hannah wasn't going to mess it up.

"Do you want to go with me? It's right in there," Hannah said, hooking her arm around the doorway and pointing toward the kitchen at the other end of the hallway.

Ashley stood frozen in place. A look of fear filled her eyes, and Hannah knew what she was thinking. "It's okay, Ash. They're all really nice here."

Tears threatened to escape as Hannah thought about her words. She'd been stranded and all alone in the middle of nowhere and these people had come to her rescue. In all honesty, Maple Glen was the kind of place Hannah had always dreamed of while growing up in Chicago. It was easy to think of a place unlike the city. One that wasn't full of noise and pollution lining the streets.

"How long have you been here?" Ashley asked, looking around at their surroundings.

Hannah knew it wasn't a laughing matter, but she chuckled anyway. She wanted to say 'too long,' but that seemed a bit dramatic and unappreciative. "Almost a month."

"Hannah," Ashley said, looking straight into Hannah's eyes, "I'm sorry I took off. I'm so sorry."

Seeing Ashley break in front of her was enough to make Hannah fall apart. She hated seeing people cry.

"It's okay," Hannah said, once again assuring her sister that everything would be okay once they got everything figured out and taken care of. Hannah couldn't promise things would change overnight. No matter how much she prayed and begged God, Hannah knew it was going to take days... months... even years. Alcoholism was an ongoing battle, and it ran deep in their family.

"We'll get through this, Ash. I promise," Hannah said, wrapping her arms around Ashley and pulling her close.

She wanted nothing but the best for her sister, and if that meant staying by her side and getting her the help she needed, that was exactly what Hannah would do.

Ashley looked over Hannah's shoulder in the direction of the kitchen doorway. Hannah knew that she was gathering the courage to make her way down the hall and into the kitchen in order to see her baby girl.

Hannah wanted her to see Grace. She wanted her to see the little girl and be thankful that Hannah had taken care of her while knowing that Grace was going to be okay.

"Do you want to see her?" Hannah asked, holding an outstretched hand in her sister's direction. "It'll be okay. I promise."

Her sister slowly nodded and took a hold of Hannah's hand. Ashley allowed Hannah to guide her toward the kitchen, and when they reached the doorway, Hannah looked back and made sure that her sister was ready.

She wasn't sure what to expect once they entered the kitchen, but deep down she knew that it would be okay. That whatever obstacles were presented, they would overcome them and defeat them.

Hannah pressed her hand against the door separating them from the others and gave her sister's hand a gentle squeeze. "You've got this. You can do this, okay?"

Ashley nodded. Whatever demons she had been battling seemed to taunt her as she feared the worst.

Hannah took a deep breath, encouraging her sister to do the same. She knew that her sister didn't like large crowds or a room full of people. She knew walking into the kitchen and seeing Vince, Cara, and the two girls might be too much, but one step at a time... they would get through it together.

LISTENING TO ASHLEY TALK ABOUT HER nights on the streets of Chicago put Hannah's problems to shame.

Hannah was more than thankful that her sister had made it out of the city alive and without further injury. She would need time to recover from the emotional trauma she'd experienced, and not to mention going through the alcoholism withdrawals, too.

Vince had offered to take Ashley to the hospital if that's what was agreed upon. The weather hadn't let up, and the snow was still falling down, leaving a white blanket covering the ground.

Hannah rode along in the backseat. Sitting right

next to Grace and her sister. They cried and hugged and cried even more.

If Hannah were to be honest, the ride to the hospital wasn't the hardest part. The hardest thing she ever had to do was take her sister's baby out of Ashley's arms and watch as the hospital staff admitted her sister to a room. Somehow that was even harder than taking Grace and leaving town after she'd been abandoned.

Grace was still too young to know what was happening, but Hannah knew that the baby felt the separation instantaneously by the way she reached out and twisted in Hannah's arms.

With one last wave goodbye, eyes full of tears and while silently praying for the best, Hannah turned and headed for the exit with Grace in her arms.

Chapter Twenty-Four

CARTER COULDN'T STOP THINKING ABOUT Hannah. She hadn't texted him. Hadn't called to tell him that she had changed her mind and that she was on her way back.

Nothing.

He couldn't send her another message, could he? Not without bugging her, right?

He wasn't good at this sort of thing and he wished he could figure out a way to make it easier.

He'd closed the shop early the other day, taking the day off after having a night out with Charlie. He didn't regret spending time with his brother. He only wished it would have been Hannah instead.

But, today was a new day and cars needed fixing. He couldn't sit around and wait to hear from Hannah when there wasn't a guarantee that she was thinking of him... let alone missing him.

The shop door opened, causing the bells above it to chime. Carter wasn't expecting anyone, but he would call himself lucky if it was Hannah.

He shook his head to clear that thought from his mind. There was no way that she would show up at his shop when she hadn't even responded to his messages.

"Hey," a voice called out before the person it belonged to rounded the corner.

"Ethan, what are you doin' here? I thought you'd be taking the day off and stayin' in where it's warm."

Ethan shook his head. "Not when there's so many hormones filling that house and emotions are running high."

Carter paused in his work and glanced over at Ethan. He wasn't sure what the guy was talking about. And he wasn't sure if he wanted to know either.

But, just like with everything else, curiosity got the best of him so he had to ask, "What's goin' on at the house that has my sister's emotions running wild?"

Ethan chuckled. "It's not just your sister, man."

Carter pushed off the front of the car he'd been working on. He wiped the grease off his hands and tossed the rag on top of the car's engine. "I guess I'm not quite sure what it is you're not tellin' me."

Ethan offered a smug grin and said, "You really don't have a clue, do you?"

Carter was about to go rounds with the guy if he didn't hurry up and spit it out already. He wasn't sure what he had missed in the days since Hannah left town, and honestly, he wasn't too concerned. He had needed the distraction that working on cars gave him.

It gave him less time to check his phone for missed calls and messages.

"Hannah's sister showed up at the bed and breakfast," Ethan explained. "Vince brought—"

"Wait," Carter said, holding up a hand and stopping Ethan from saying another word. Carter didn't care to hear how Ashley got there. "Does Hannah know? Where's Ashley now? Is she still at the house?"

Ethan raised his hands and motioned for Carter to take it easy. Carter dug his phone out of his pocket and prepared to dial Hannah's number. If her sister was in town, she had every right to know and she needed to come back. If not for him, at least for her sister.

"She's already here," Ethan said, once again motioning for Carter to stop and listen. "Hannah, I mean."

"Hannah?"

Ethan nodded. "She never left town. She's been here the whole time. Since the storm hit and then her sister showed up—"

Carter didn't let Ethan finish his sentence. He gathered his phone and truck keys before high tailing it out of the shop.

If Hannah never left town and she was still at the bed and breakfast, and Ashley had shown up with Vince... then she had a lot on her plate, and Carter wanted to be there for her.

Taking the back roads to his sister's bed and breakfast, Carter had time to think about what he would do once he arrived at the house. He hated the fact that he hadn't known Hannah never left town. He hated it even more knowing that she hadn't responded back to his messages.

He could take partial blame in the whole situation. He could have tried harder to prove how much he cared about her. How much he loved her. *Love.* The word that had once left a bitter, resentful feeling inside of him now seemed to open a sense of hope and understanding. He wanted nothing but the best for Hannah and Grace. He loved them both.

Carter guided the truck along the road and slowed as he neared the entrance to the bed and breakfast. He glanced at the house, decked out in Christmas lights and yard decorations, as he pulled into the driveway.

It was hard to believe that Christmas was right around the corner. For the first time in years, it didn't feel like Christmas. Holidays were a big thing in the Mitchell family. They had several traditions put together by Carter's mother and his aunt Fran. Over the years, new traditions were born, but the old still remained.

Carter thought of the town's festival on Main Street that occured year after year since he was a child. He wasn't sure if it was coming up this weekend or the following, but he wanted to take Hannah and Grace to it.

He shifted the truck into park and stared at the house. He wasn't sure what to expect once he got inside. He needed a plan B just in case Hannah didn't want him there, though he desperately hoped that wasn't the case.

Killing the engine, he hopped out of his truck and took a deep breath in an attempt to calm his nerves. He wasn't a fan of forcing himself into a situation where he wasn't wanted, but he needed Hannah in his life, and he could only hope that she needed him in hers just as much.

Walking toward the house, Carter took the steps two at a time and knocked on the door. He heard Ethan's truck behind him, pulling into the driveway as he waited for someone to answer the door.

The wooden door opened, and his sister greeted him with a shake of her head. "If I told you a million times, you still wouldn't listen," she said, opening the door wider and inviting him in. "You don't have to knock—"

"Where's Hannah?"

The house was eerily quiet, and he glanced around for any sign of Hannah or the baby. He headed for the stairs, but Catie stopped him. Taking a hold of the sleeve of his coat, Catie said, "They're not back yet."

It was only then that he saw the look on Catie's face. Something had happened. "From where? What happened? Ethan said that everyone was here. That Ashley came—"

"She did," Catie said with a nod, "but after Hannah talked with her for a while, they agreed to let Vince take her to the hospital. Ashley agreed to start rehab as long as Hannah promised to take care of Grace."

Carter's heart sank. If he had known that Hannah was still in town. If he had known that Ashley was there... He would have been there for Hannah. For Grace. He wanted to be there now. Wherever they were, he wanted to be there.

"But they're for sure coming back?" He gripped his keys in his hand and turned toward the door. "What hospital did they take her to?"

He wasn't sure if his old truck would make it out of town, but he would try. If trying meant that he could be with Hannah and Grace... he would do anything for them.

"They should be on their way back by now," Catie said. She walked toward the living room and motioned for Carter to take a seat. The last thing he wanted to do was sit and wait. He hated waiting while knowing that Hannah and Grace had just gone through yet another life-changing event and they needed someone there for them. "They should be here soon. Do you want anything to eat or drink? Are you hungry?"

Carter shook his head. What he wanted was for his girls to be there, safe and sound in his arms. He wanted Hannah to know that he was going to be there for them as long as she would let him.

~

AFTER AN HOUR OF WAITING AND SENDING messages back and forth, Hannah walked through the front door with Grace in her arms.

Carter jumped from the chair he'd been sitting in for what felt like forever and met her in the entryway.

"Hannah," he said, offering to take Grace and removing the little girl's hat and mittens before unzipping her coat. He held tightly to Grace as he watched Hannah go through the motions of taking her coat off and hanging it on a nearby hook. Mascara-stained tears streaked her cheeks as she turned to face him. Hannah stepped toward him, walking right into his open arms and buried her face into his chest. He wrapped his girls into a tight hug and said, "I'm sorry. If I had known... If I hadn't been so stubborn..."

"I can't do this," Hannah whispered, her voice cracking with emotion. "I hated dropping her off at the hospital, Carter. Like she was a prisoner and had done something terribly wrong and needs to be punished. The look on her face..."

He didn't know what to say to make the situation better. He'd never had to experience anything like that in his twenty-two years of living, but he did know one thing, and that was the fact that Hannah was a strong woman and she would be able to get through it. Whether she chose to do so on her own or with him by her side, she would get through it. *They* would get through it.

"She's going to be okay, Han," he whispered as he tried his best to comfort her. "And you will be, too. She's getting the help she needs, and it's only a matter of time before she's back home and with you again."

"I should've never left her alone like that," Hannah said as sobs wracked through her, causing her to shake in his arms. Grace fidgeted, and he knew that she was getting tired of being held. He glanced over his shoulder in search of Catie, not wanting to let go of Hannah. Thankfully, Catie was nearby and able to take Grace so he could focus solely on Hannah for the time being. Everything else could wait. "I left her, and she had no choice but to turn to drugs and alcohol..."

"No, that's not true, Han," he said, knowing for a fact that it wasn't fair for her to take the blame for her sister's actions. "She chose to leave first. She left you and Grace in search of those things. You can't be the one to take the blame for that. She chose to do what she did, and you had no choice but to do what you thought was best."

Hannah straightened in his arms and looked him in the eye. Her makeup was smudged and streaked with tears, but she was still the beautiful woman he'd fallen for. She was still the woman he'd met and knew from day one that she was going to change his mind about love and giving it another chance. "She looked so rough, Carter," Hannah said, tears welling in her eyes and threatening to escape. "I hardly recognized her. If it hadn't been for her eyes and the way she said my name..."

Carter pulled Hannah in close, trying his best to comfort her. He couldn't find the words to say, so he just remained quiet as he held her in his arms. Sometimes words weren't needed in a time like this. He knew that what Hannah needed was someone to be there for her, and that was exactly what he was going to do.

"Thank you," she whispered, pressing her head against his chest.

"You don't have to thank me, Han," he said. "I'm here because I care. I'm doing what I am because I..."

His words trailed off as he thought of what he truly wanted to say. He had so much he wanted to tell her, but he had never been a man of many words. She needed to know that he was there for her and that he would never leave her side. She needed to know that for as long as she was in Maple Glen, she had nothing to worry about.

"Hannah," he said softly as he took a step back. She looked up at him, and he could see the hurricane of emotions rolling through her eyes. He wanted nothing more than to take away the hurt and the pain that her life had caused. Carter traced a finger along her jawline while keeping his eyes locked on hers. "I should've been here sooner, and I'm sorry that I wasn't. I figured that you'd left town and weren't coming back, but that was my mistake for assuming that based on my past."

She nodded slowly, her eyes filled with tears as he tucked a loose strand of hair behind her ear.

"I can't promise you that things are going to be easy," Carter said, "but I can promise you that I will be right here by your side for as long as you'll let me."

Hannah kept her eyes on his and nodded softly. She deserved more than what life had given her. She deserved happiness and freedom while knowing that she had security and a place to call home.

"I know that I'm not a man of many words and I suck at this kind of thing," he said with a light chuckle. He was relieved when her lips pulled into a soft smile as she looked up at him. "But I just want you to know that as long as you're here, you'll always have people who care about you and want the best for you."

He paused long enough to see her nod before saying, "You'll always have me and a place to call home. I'll take care of you and Grace and be there for the both of you. We can take it one day at a time."

Hannah's lips parted as though she were going to say something, but instead, she smiled and her eyes lit up. For the first time in a while, Carter watched as she relaxed and let go of everything she'd been carrying.

"Hannah," he said, tracing her jawline with his thumb as he thought about what he was going to say next. He could only hope that he didn't sound like a fool when he said it. Taking a deep breath, he tried his best to relax and said, "When I first met you, I was quite sure that I'd never love again... but you proved me wrong."

She quirked a brow, but remained quiet, silently encouraging him to continue.

"I've never met a woman I've cared about as much as I do about you," he admitted, his cheeks warming as he grinned. "And I won't even mention Grace."

Hannah let out a soft laugh and shook her head. He loved hearing Hannah's laugh. He would make it his job to hear that everyday for the rest of his life.

"That one had me wrapped around her tiny little finger since day one," he admitted, "and the two of you together is what makes me whole."

Hannah's eyes lit up as a smile spread across her face. "Do you mean that?"

"I mean everything I say," Carter said, "and I wouldn't say anything I didn't mean."

"Carter," Hannah said, taking a step back and looking up at him with a concerned look on her face. "I'm not sure if I should say this. Maybe it's too early or maybe I'm wrong..."

He wasn't sure what to expect. The thought of her telling him that she didn't want him in her life crossed his mind, but he didn't want to believe it. He had enough doubt running through his mind about being able to love someone enough to make them stay, he didn't need to add to it.

A tear fell and streamed down her face as she

looked him in the eye. A soft smile spread across her face as she said, "I love you, Carter."

"Do you mean that?" he asked with a grin.

"I wouldn't say things I didn't mean."

Carter lifted her chin with his finger and met her lips with his.

"That's good, because I love you, too."

Chapter Twenty-Five

IT WASN'T EASY GETTING THROUGH THE DAYS while knowing her sister was in rehab and Christmas was approaching. It would be the first Christmas without Ashley around, but Catie promised Hannah that Ashley would be okay and having her in rehab was the best for Ashley and Grace.

Carter had spent the night at the bed and breakfast each night and had asked Hannah to be prepared for the fun events lined up for the rest of the week.

She wasn't quite sure what that meant, but first, Catie wanted to take them to Fran's Coffee and treat them to girl talk while the guys hung out at the house and busied themselves with hanging more Christmas lights.

As Hannah placed Grace's car seat in the backseat next to Alex, who was on winter break from school and both Grant and Cassie were working, she overheard Carter grumbling to Ethan about hanging so many Christmas lights and making some kind of reference to *National Lampoon's Christmas Vacation.*

She laughed as she shut the back door and called out, "We should watch that movie later... unless you prefer to watch *The Grinch* instead?"

Carter laughed and shook his head as he waved them goodbye. "Go drink coffee and have fun with the girls."

Hannah smiled and waved as she slid into the passenger seat of Catie's car. "Ready?" Catie asked with a smile.

"Ready!" Alex shouted from the backseat, causing Hannah to crack up.

"I'm with her," Hannah said, hooking a thumb over her shoulder with a smile. "I'm as ready as I'll ever be."

Catie shifted the car into drive and pulled out of the driveway. "I hope so, because Aunt Fran's going to be thrilled to hear that you've decided to stay *and* that her matchmaking might have worked yet again."

"What's her story, anyway?" Hannah asked. It was something she'd been wondering since she had first met Fran. She hadn't seen a ring on her finger, and no one mentioned whether or not Fran was living her own happily ever after.

Catie smiled, but remained quiet as she guided the

car along the curves of the backroad and into town. Hannah knew there was something secretive going on, but she had a feeling it would come out eventually. She knew from her own experience that things in a small town didn't stay unknown for too long.

"You might just have to ask Fran about that," Catie said with a light chuckle. She turned onto Main Street and pulled up in front of the coffee shop. She put her car in park and looked over at Hannah. Hannah sat quietly in her spot, looking out through the snow-covered windshield and wondered why the match-maker hadn't been matched.

"I just might, but first, I need coffee," Hannah said, opening her door and climbing out before grabbing Grace from the backseat. "Grace has to be teething. She was awake most of the night. I'm going to need a pot of coffee just to get through the day."

Catie laughed as she helped Alex from the back-seat. Alex took off in a mad dash for the door, calling out something about racing them and the last one in being a rotten egg. Hannah laughed as she walked alongside Catie.

Catie had become the kind of friend that Hannah had always wanted in her life. Aside from Tara, Hannah never had a good friend she could count on when times were hard. Hannah was thankful that she'd met Catie when she did and that they were well on their way to a lasting friendship.

"Well, look who it is," Fran called out as the bells

above the door jingled when they entered. "I heard through the grapevine that you've decided to stay in Maple Glen after all?"

Fran walked toward them, arms open wide as she approached Hannah. She walked into Fran's arms and welcomed the much-needed hug. She hadn't seen Fran in what felt like forever, but now that she knew she was staying put, she'd see Fran more often.

"Word travels fast in small towns, ya know?" Fran said, patting Hannah on the back and turning her attention to Grace. Hannah removed Grace's hat and mittens. "And look who we have here," she said, tracing a finger over Grace's cheek.

"She might not be too chipper this morning," Hannah said with a frown. "I think she's teething."

"Oh, you poor little thing," Fran said, softly kissing the top of the baby's head. Fran smiled at Alex before wrapping her in her arms. "How are you? I hear that you have a Christmas recital comin' up soon."

Alex nodded enthusiastically and said, "Uh huh. *The Nutcracker*."

Fran grinned ear to ear. Hannah enjoyed watching the interaction between Fran and the littles. She was such a kind hearted woman who made time for everyone.

"I'll be there," Fran said, booping Alex on the nose and causing a fit of laughter to escape Alex. "Front and center. I wouldn't miss it for the world."

Hannah unzipped her coat and hung it on a nearby hook.

"How about you girls go on over to the booth and I'll bring you some coffee," Fran offered, motioning them to have a seat. As they made their way to the booth, the others smiled and waved, scooting over to make room for them to sit down. "I'll be right back," Fran called out over her shoulder before disappearing behind the counter.

Only when she came back, the girls fell silent at the table. Fran looked at each of them and asked, "What'd I miss?"

She handed mugs to each of them and offered refills to the others as she kept a wary eye on them. "Someone tell me why you got quiet as soon as I walked up."

Hannah glanced around the table and realized that no one was going to ask Fran *the* question, and no one wanted to know more than Hannah did, so she said, "Okay, I'll ask."

Fran slid into the booth opposite of Hannah and waited for her to ask the question everyone was dying to know the answer to.

"Now that you've run out of people to match, when are *you* going to fall in love?"

Fran smiled ear to ear, and Hannah knew that she was going to skillfully avoid the question. In true Fran fashion, the middle-aged woman said, "If I were to be honest, which I am, there will always be an opportunity to play matchmaker."

She took a sip from her coffee and smiled at Hannah. "Whether it be one plus two, like it was in your case, or another situation, there will always be love waiting to be found."

Epilogue

Hannah bundled Grace up in her winter gear and headed out to Carter's truck. Today was the day the Mitchell family got together and gathered at the tree farm outside of town. Carter had told Hannah all about it, explaining to her that it was a day of fun while his family members picked out their Christmas trees and hauled them back home—well, *homes*, now that they're all grown.

There were several festivities and events to prep the townspeople for the upcoming holiday, from the chili supper at the little white church on the corner of Main Street to the lighting of the large evergreen tree in the center of town.

"I hope you know this is going to be the best day ever," Carter said, helping Hannah buckle Grace into her car seat.

Hannah smiled and said, "So I've heard, and I can't wait."

She had yet to meet the whole Mitchell family, but if they were anything like Catie, Carter, and Cara, then she had nothing to worry about. The Mitchell family so far had been welcoming and so inviting, and Hannah couldn't thank them enough.

Hannah couldn't wait to see the tree farm. She'd never been to one and had only seen them in the Christmas movies she watched on the Hallmark channel. She couldn't help but feel like she'd been cast into one of those movies, with Carter playing the unsuspecting hero and her as the overly giddy heroine who had a future full of hope and dreams as she overcame her past filled with uncertainty.

She smiled at the thought.

"There it is," Carter said, pointing to Hannah's right where evergreen trees lined a field surrounded by families as they picked out the perfect tree for their homes. "We come here every year in hopes of finding just the right tree. Not too tall and not too short, but just right."

Hannah laughed when she thought of calling him out the other day about being the next Clark Griswold in *National Lampoon's Christmas Vacation*. It all made perfect sense now that she put the pieces together. "I knew you weren't the Grinch," she said, smiling over at him and laughing when he tried his best to imitate the Grinch but failed. "Nice try, though."

Carter pulled into an empty spot and parked. Thankfully, the weather had straightened up and the sun decided to peek out from behind the clouds. It was an ideal day to be outside to pick out a Christmas tree.

Hannah carried Grace as she walked alongside Carter toward the entrance of the tree farm. A tall man wearing a cowboy hat stood to the side, greeting everyone as they made their way through the makeshift gate.

"Hey, Curt," Carter said, offering the man his hand with a firm shake. Hannah watched the exchange and wondered how long Carter had known Curt. "Long time, no see. How's the ranch holdin' up in Montana?"

"Well, it's holdin' up pretty well," Curt said. "In fact, I've got my boys runnin' it right now just so I could come back to Maple Glen and take care of the trees for Christmas."

Hannah noted that the man was middle-aged and polite. He seemed friendly and laid back, almost as though he fit right in with the Mitchell family.

"And who's this?" Curt asked, turning his attention to Hannah and Grace. "You've finally found someone to settle down with?"

Carter cleared his throat and placed a hand on Hannah's lower back. "This is Hannah Michaelson and Grace."

Hannah noticed the way Carter took the time to introduce them to the man, telling him about how they met. At the end of Carter's story, Curt slapped a hand on Carter's shoulder and said, "Thatta boy. It was good seein' ya. Now go on and get you and your *plus two* a tree for Christmas."

Carter nodded once and guided Hannah and Grace to the selection of trees. Hannah had a feeling it wouldn't take long to pick one out, especially since her eyes gravitated toward one right away. "I like this one," she pointed out. She hadn't thought too much about where the tree would go since she was still staying at the bed and breakfast, but maybe if she was lucky, Carter would let her take it back with her.

"That one?" Carter said with a slight grunt. "But you haven't seen the rest of 'em."

Hannah shrugged. "Sometimes you just know that it's the one."

Carter opened his mouth to say something, but laughter echoed from somewhere behind them and pulled their attention away from one another to find the source.

Fran was standing at the gate with Curt, talking and laughing like they were old friends. Hannah smiled at the interaction.

"They seem to be picking up right where they left off," Carter whispered, and Hannah picked up on the fact that he was being careful not to say it too loudly.

"Are they old friends?" Hannah asked, intrigued by what Carter wasn't saying. She watched in awe at the interaction between Curt and Fran. If someone didn't know about their past, like Hannah, it would be safe to assume they shared quite a connection with each other.

"Somethin' like that," Carter said and turned back to the tree Hannah had picked out. "What do you say we cut down this tree and take it home?"

"Home? Like back to the bed and breakfast?" she teased, shocked when he shook his head. "No?"

"Nope," he said with a smirk. "I've got another place in mind."

Her heart skipped a beat and she felt like the whole world had stopped spinning. A breath hitched in her throat, knowing there could only be one place Carter had in mind.

"I've already got a room set up for Grace," he said, setting down the hand saw and taking a step toward her. "It isn't much, but it'll do for now. I just figured that since you're stayin' in town, you might as well have a place to call home, and there isn't a place better than mine."

Hannah released the breath she'd been holding and said, "Okay."

"Okay?" he asked as a look of shock crossed his face. It was obvious that he hadn't planned on Hannah agreeing to move in with him. She wasn't sure what to expect, but he was right, she deserved a place to call home—and so did Grace.

She nodded and pointed toward the tree.

"Let's get this tree cut down and head home," she said.

Carter pulled her in close to him, the warmth of his breath on her nose as she stared up at him. Staring into his eyes, she saw only sincerity and comfort. She couldn't wait to see what the future held for the two of them, and Grace, if she was lucky and her sister decided to let them adopt her. But none of that was important right now.

All that mattered now was that they were together and they had each other. All because her car broke down and had stranded her, leaving her no choice but to fall in love with Maple Glen and the man who fixed her car.

Enjoy what you've read?
Continue reading the series now!
Christmas for Two

A Note From The Author

If you enjoyed reading One plus Two, please consider leaving a review.

Thank you!

About the Author

Christina Butrum launched her writing career in 2015 with the release of The Fairshore Series.

Writing contemporary fiction, she brings realistic situations with swoon-worthy romance to the pages - allowing her readers to fall in love right along with the characters.

When she isn't busy writing, Christina enjoys spending time with her family. Christina Butrum looks forward to publishing many more books for her readers to enjoy.

www.authorchristinabutrum.com

Sign Up for Christina's Newsletter Here: https://www.subscribepage.com/authorcbutrum
Join Christina's Group Here: https://www.facebook.com/groups/ButrumsBookBabes

- facebook.com/authorcbutrum
- twitter.com/authorcbutrum
- instagram.com/authorcbutrum
- amazon.com/author/christinabutrum
- bookbub.com/profile/christina-butrum

Also by Christina Butrum

FAIRSHORE SERIES

Second Chances

Unexpected Chances

Fair Chances

KATE'S DUET

Kate's Valentine

Kate's Forever

CEDAR VALLEY SERIES

All She Ever Wanted

Everything She Needed

All She Ever Desired

A MAPLE GLEN ROMANCE SERIES

It Takes Two

Coffee for Two

RSVP for Two

Room for Two

Lesson for Two

One plus Two

Christmas for Two

DIXON RANCH SERIES

The Cowboy's Home

The Cowboy's Heart

The Cowboy's Hope

STANDALONE NOVELS

No Place Like Home - Love in Seattle

Saving Jenna

INTERCONNECTED NOVELLA

Sweet on Love - A Lover's Landing Novella

SWEET PROMISE PRESS NOVELS

Choosing Chelsea - A Gold Coast Retrievers Novel

No Time for Goodbyes - A No Brides Club Novel

No Time for Mistletoe - A No Brides Club Novel

Made in United States
North Haven, CT
17 January 2025

64545774R00143